The Angel Box

The Angel Box

YAUNA HANSEN-SMITH

Designed by Vince Pannullo
Printed in the United States of America by RJ Communications.

ISBN: 978-0-578-15083-3

Dedication

TO my mother Annabelle Hansen who had an insatiable appetite for the written word. She inspired me with her self taught knowledge and wisdom. She was a wonderful human being to all that knew her, constantly loved and always missed.

Preface

1792

SHE awakes to her own moaning; a racking pain envelopes her entire body. Her mind wanders, trying to grasp her torrid surroundings. She is high atop sticks and hay tied to a crude platform.

Smoke stings her eyes. She coughs, trying to clear her lungs, but to no avail. The crowd below jeers at her, their laughter deafening. Why are they laughing? Why won't they help? There are others screaming in agony. Just then, a crow swoops down and opens a deep gash above her left eye. Blood drips down to her lips, tasting like metal in her mouth. Swarms of crows fill the sky, swooping in and out of the insanity; their cawing is deafening. The fire licks at her feet as the mob jeers and mocks them. Rats run through the sea of people, but no one notices. The crowd is in a frenzy now, as if mad. Then the Wolves come. They stock slowly, while white foam oozes from their mouths, gnashing their fangs at anything in their path. People run in terror. The Wolves circle around the fire, then sit and wait. And still the screams of the victims cry out.

This must be a nightmare, she thinks, wondering why she can't wake up. The fire burns her flesh. She looks down at her arm; the skin bubbles up and rips away, leaving streaks of red.

Smoke is thick in her lungs; she can't quit coughing. She tries to scream but can't. Then she remembers... They cut out her tongue.

Chapter 1

PRESENT TIME

JULIANNA ran up the stairs to the veranda. She felt sick, unable to control her sobs. How could he do that to her? She trusted him. Now everything was a lie. She crumpled down on a chair and looked up at the night sky. The stars were brilliant, like a million diamonds against a black canvas. Tears streamed down her face. She wondered if she should leave him. Of course she still loved him. There had to be an explanation. *He's not like this*, she thought. But something else was really strange; she felt it down to her very soul. Eric was becoming more and more distant, and at times he was a total disconnect. He'd just stare at her like he didn't know her. It was a side of him she'd never seen, and it terrified her.

It all started about five months ago. She and Eric had been invited to her publisher's house. All the newest authors that had signed with Whitworth and Johnson Publishing had been invited. Eric wasn't particularly excited to go, but when his client canceled out of a meeting on a potential sale of the Newlington Estate, he begrudgingly agreed. Eric thought Julianna's love of writing was just a silly phase until she signed with one of the largest publishing houses in North America. Julianna loved to write short novels about fantasy, mainly for children. Now her passion had grown to extensive research on historic families in Salem, Massachusetts, possibly for a romance novel.

At the party, she discussed her idea with Lauren. She and Lauren had become good friends as well as colleagues. Lauren Harrison was from England and listened intently, her big blue eyes taking in every detail as Julianna spoke. Lauren looked up to Julianna, and she admired her greatly. Julianna sold more children's books in one year than many authors had done in a lifetime.

"I'm hungry, Julianna," Lauren laughed as she stood up, embarrassed by her grumbling stomach. "The nosh looks brilliant!"

Julianna watched as Lauren's slender frame walked across the oriental carpet to the dining room table full of hors d'oeuvres. Lauren looked back at her, gesturing to ask her if she wanted some. Of course, she nodded, laughing. Lauren's teeth shone bright against her tan, and her long dark hair hung straight down to her waist. She wore a simple black dress with sparkled flip flops. All Julianna could think of as Lauren walked back with the hors d'oeuvres was the diet she was going to start tomorrow. Julianna and Lauren continued chatting about story ideas as they devoured the delicious food.

Then something suddenly crashed in the dining room. They both jumped and turned to see Eric bent down helping a curvaceous blonde to her feet. A champagne glass had shattered under the table and a maid was quickly sweeping it into a dust pan. The petite blonde stood up and grabbed Eric's face and planted a kiss fiercely on his lips then thanked him and brushed his hair from his eyes. Julianna turned away seething.

She looked at Lauren who was standing with her mouth agape. "That daft cow," Lauren muttered.

Eric walked up behind and squeezed Julianna's shoulders "Guess what?" he said excitedly.

"What?" Her dark brown eyes glared at him.

"What..." He could tell she was irritated and laughed. "Honey, she's a foreigner. That's what they do. She's my client, the one who canceled today. Come on, you're mad at me?"

She scoffed, "You're so naive Eric," shaking her head.

"The one who's buying the Newlington Estate," he continued. "That's Anya Thorsen."

A look of disbelief crossed both Julianna and Lauren's faces. Julianna thought the petite blonde looked familiar. "You mean the actress?"

"Yes," he excitedly replied.

Julianna glanced across the room and saw Anya sitting on a lush green velvet couch sipping champagne, surrounded by admirers vying for her attention. Anya suddenly turned her head as if she knew Eric and Julianna were talking about her. She stared at them, her emerald eyes transfixed on their every move. Then she smiled, exposing her dazzling white teeth and beckoning them over.

Julianna and Eric excused themselves from Lauren and crossed the parlor to the living room. Julianna felt giddy as they walked across the oriental rug into the living room where Anya was seated. She had never met a celebrity before and was star struck. Eric made the introductions, and Anya held out her delicate, perfect hand which had the biggest diamond on it Julianna had ever seen.

Anya noticed and was amused by her reaction. Giggling, she said, "It's just a ring. My boyfriend Dominic gave it to me. I think he meant for it to be an engagement ring."

She beckoned Julianna closer and whispered, "He's not

too happy I'm wearing it on my right hand... C'est la vie." She laughed.

Julianna had never seen such a beautiful person in her life. Anya was flawless; she was like a beautiful painting that Michelangelo or Rafael had created. Julianna was speechless and made small talk, but she noticed Eric's gaze on herself instead of Anya. She was a contrast to Anya, but beautiful nonetheless. Her long auburn hair fell in long curls to the middle of her back, as she nervously adjusted her shoulder strap on her dress. Her coloring was olive tone with dark brown eyes slanted up at the corners giving her an exotic look. Yet Anya did have an extraordinary charisma. Her clever banter captivated everyone.

Later that night as she and Eric drove back to their apartment, they both sighed.

"Isn't she great?" Eric beamed.

"Yeah...but that kiss still bugs me."

"Oh come on," Eric laughed. "She's a--"

"I know, she's a foreigner. That's what they do," Julianna piped in.

"Exactly," he said. "She is nice though."

Julianna grinned. "She really is and..."

"Rich," Eric added. "This sale is the sale of a lifetime. We're asking 120 million for the Newlington Estate."

Julianna choked on the shrimp puff she was eating, which she carefully tucked back into a napkin and stuffed into her purse.

"You're kidding... What's your commission?"

"Five percent on this one," Eric replied. He winked, then let out a yell. "You know what? We're not going to discuss this anymore. We might jinx it."

Julianna laughed. "Eric I've never known you to be superstitious."

"I'm not...I'm just saying let's not talk about it anymore."

"Okay," Julianna grinned.

They got to their apartment and crawled into bed, both exhausted. Eric was snoring as soon as his head hit the pillow. She gazed at her handsome husband, his curly brown hair, his scruffy 5 o'clock shadow, and his sweet sleepy eyes. She loved everything about him: his strong features and athletic physique. He'd been quite the basketball player--division one point guard at Stanford. But due to an ankle injury, his NBA career goal ended, and he started his real estate business.

Julianna was very tired but had been unable to sleep since they'd moved to Salem. She tossed and turned all night. Once again her sleep was fitful, never remembering her dreams.

Chapter 2

THE day after the party, Julianna dove into her research. The Ericksons were the original homesteaders in Salem. They were also the wealthiest and still had family living in a beautiful mansion not far from town. Much of the real estate in town and Laurs, a high end department store, was owned by the Ericksons. All the wealthiest people of Langendorf, a suburb of Salem, shopped for designer clothing, furniture and fine china there.

Julianna's research took her to the Langendorf Library where she went to the archives. She found old pictures of horse drawn carriages, men in top hats and starched suits, and women in dark clothes with their hair severely pulled back in tight buns.

The library was eerily silent. No one was there except the creepy librarian behind the counter.

As Julianna continued her research, she found volumes of old newspaper clippings. The yellowed pages were fragile, and she was afraid they were going to disintegrate in her hands. She carefully turned to a page that had an article about a debutante ball. Part of the article was missing as if it had been torn out.

That's odd, Julianna thought as she looked at the faded picture.

She got her magnifying glass out and pondered over the news clipping. The picture was of a blond-haired debutante from 1792 named Emily Erickson. She was just sixteen years old, but the similarity made Julianna shudder. She looked shockingly like Anya, and from the picture Emily seemed to be looking right back at her. Julianna gasped and jumped in her seat, dropping the magnifying glass on the table. The loud thud echoed through the enormous volumes of dusty manuscripts perched high on the huge book shelves.

She heard clicking heels on the tiled floor loom closer as the creepy librarian briskly walked towards her. Her lips were pursed, clearly irritated.

"Is everything alright," the librarian snapped. Her sharp features and hair tautly pulled back in a bun made her look manic.

Julianna looked around; still no one was there.

Why is she so mad, she thought.

"Uh, sorry," Julianna blushed, gathering her belongings to head out the door.

Wait, she thought, *if Eric is ever going to believe this I have to have proof. I need a copy of that news clipping.*

She quietly walked back to the librarian's desk and whispered about getting a copy of the news clipping. The librarian looked annoyed as she promptly went into the next room and came out with a manila envelope that she handed to Julianna.

"That will be one dollar," she said, pursing her lips, then forcing a smile.

Julianna handed her a dollar, turned and walked out the large glass doors. Then she started down the long cobblestone stairway to the street below. She pulled out the picture.

Oh no, she thought. The picture was different. Only the back of Emily Erickson's head was showing. She must have scanned the wrong one.

She turned and started back up towards the library and was almost to the top when she felt something swish the back of her head. She whirled around as a crow dove down, knocking her down the stairs. Everything went flying out of her hands as she tumbled down, smashing her head and landing on the sidewalk below. Her whole body was racked with pain. She managed to open her eyes and saw crows perched high above on the eaves of the historic building, their caws deafening as their beady eyes stared down at her.

People...unfamiliar faces asking her if she was alright...then she lost consciousness.

Chapter 3

JULIANNA awoke to her own moaning; the pain in her head was excruciating. Her entire body throbbed. Her head was spinning as she tried to focus and sit up. The room was dim with candle light. *Is it night?* she wondered. And again she fell into a deep sleep. Hours later, she regained consciousness and felt someone wiping her forehead, only to fall asleep again.

Finally, she awoke to a warm soft breeze fluttering though the lace curtains. She smelled lilacs and coffee. Someone was cooking. She smelled bacon and ham. Her stomach rumbled. *When did I eat last?* Her stomach felt as if it was laying flat on her backbone. She was starving. She smelled buttered toast and potatoes. She heard birds chirping and people talking in hushed tones. She slowly opened her eyes. It was bright. She blinked, trying to accustom her eyes to the glare.

"She's awake. She's opening her eyes," a woman's familiar voice stated.

"Thank the good Lord," a man's voice said. She didn't recognize his voice.

As Julianna's blurred vision focused, she saw people she didn't know, strangers except for Anya who was holding her hand and smiling.

"We were so worried about you."

Anya gently kissed Julianna's cheek. Julianna tried to sit up but everything hurt, especially her head. She touched the cloth bandage that was wrapped around it.

"Where's Eric?" she muttered.

"Who?" asked the elderly gentleman.

"Eric." She saw their bewildered expressions. "My husband."

They just stared at her, then started whispering to each other.

Julianna sat up on her elbows and looked at Anya. "Where's Eric, Anya?"

"What? Honey, I'm Emily...your sister...Remember."

Julianna felt the blood drain from her face. This was incomprehensible. Panic encompassed her. She couldn't breathe.

"Where am I?" she whispered, her own voice unrecognizable. Trembling with fear, she stared at them.

"Your home, honey. Doc Briggs and I brought you here two days ago...after that terrible fall."

Julianna looked at both of them. Their clothes were outdated. The room she was in, she had never seen before.

"What kind of sick joke is this?" she screamed and started crying uncontrollably, covering her face.

Emily made everyone leave the room, even Doc Briggs. He shut the door behind him. Emily sat on the bed near Julianna's feet.

"Doc Briggs said you might have amnesia." Anya looked at her strangely.

"Listen, Anya, or Emily, or whoever you are, I don't have amnesia."

She grabbed Emily's arm, then noticed once again her clothing.

Emily jerked loose. "Listen, Victoria, I'm sorry you're hurt."

"What?" Julianna interrupted.

Emily started talking again.

"No," Julianna muttered, staring at Emily as if in a trance. "What did you call me?"

Emily looked at Julianna bewildered.

"My name...what's my name?" Julianna screamed.

"Victoria Erickson," Emily replied sullenly.

Julianna gasped; her head was spinning as she slowly rose from her bed. The flowered night gown she had on hung down to her feet. She walked to the vanity and looked at herself in the mirror. She put her hands to her face, but the face in the mirror wasn't hers. She was a different person. Julianna crumpled to the ground sobbing.

"What's happening?" she wailed.

Emily ran to the door, and Doc Briggs came in and helped Julianna back into bed. He gave her a hot drink that put her back into a deep sleep.

Chapter 4

JULIANNA began to gain consciousness again. Terrified to face the reality she was in, slowly she opened her eyes. Everything was dark except the glow from her night stand. It was her alarm clock. She let out of sigh of relief.

Just then Eric opened the door. "Hi, sleepyhead, how are you feeling?" He sat beside her on the bed.

"I'm back," she gasped.

"Yeah you've been sleeping for two days. You had quite a concussion. We tried to keep you awake but couldn't. The doctors said to let you sleep, and since there was no bleeding in your brain you'd be okay."

"No, Eric, you don't understand. I was somewhere else."

Eric looked at Julianna sympathetically.

"Quit it, I'm not crazy. It happened. I--I was in a different time...in the past."

She realized how insane that sounded, especially after a brain injury. She looked at Eric, her eyes pleading for him to believe her.

Eric laughed nervously. "Honey you were right here in this bed sleeping the entire time."

"No, Eric, I was somewhere else," she whispered.

"Well maybe because of the concussion, you were hallucinating," he responded.

"No, listen to me. I wasn't dreaming or hallucinating. Something happened. I can't explain it."

She sat up in bed, trying to make him understand. "I was in the past and I wasn't myself I was...Victoria Erickson, Emily Erickson's sister, and Emily was... Anya!"

Eric looked at Julianna in disbelief.

"Quit looking at me like I'm crazy. I'm not! It really happened."

"Okay, you need to eat."

He promptly left and brought back a tray with coffee, orange juice, buttered toast with her favorite apricot jelly, scrambled eggs, hash browns, bacon and ham. Julianna remembered the smells from before. She looked out at the crimson sunrise. A warm, soft breeze blew against the lace curtains. She smelled the lilacs outside the window and heard the musical chirping of the birds as the city sprang to life.

Maybe it was a dream, or a nightmare, she thought.

She was too hungry and worn out to dwell on it and began voraciously eating her breakfast. As she finished everything on her plate, Julianna heard a familiar voice. Then Eric opened the bedroom door and whispered, "You have a visitor."

Julianna wiped her mouth with a napkin and pulled the covers up to her chin. Eric opened the door again, and Anya walked in. Julianna jumped, her heart racing. Anya was wearing a zebra trench coat with a red diamond-encrusted belt tied tightly around her curvacious waist. Her blonde hair was pulled back in a high ponytail. She flashed her brilliant smile towards Julianna. Julianna slouched further down into her bed, wishing she could disappear altogether. Anya sat at the foot of her bed, then moved closer and softly grasped Julianna's hand.

"Everyone was so worried when they heard about your unfortunate accident, Jules," Anya whispered.

"Everyone?" Julianna questioned.

"Yes, everyone at the party was called...your publishers. You know you are the new and upcoming protege of Whitworth and Johnson. You're going to be famous."

Julianna looked at the other side of the room where dozens of bouquets sat on a table. Balloons and cards with get well wishes lined the wall. Then she looked back at Anya.

"Tell me what happened to you. How did you fall?" Anya looked concerned, and her eyes glistened as if she could cry at any moment.

"Um..." Julianna thought back to the library. She remembered the bird. "A crow knocked me down the stairs."

Anya looked horrified. "You poor, poor thing," she cooed. "Well I hope you don't mind, but I took the liberty of bringing a very dear friend with me today. He's been visiting from Sweden."

She walked over to the door and opened it. An elderly gentleman walked in. Julianna emotions went from recognition to terror. She ran to the bathroom, slammed the door, and promptly threw up.

"Julianna, are you alright?" Anya inquired.

"No, no, I'm not. I'm sorry," she sputtered.

"Well, I brought Doctor Swensen here to check on you. He's the top brain surgeon in Sweden and is giving a lecture at the University tonight," Anya stated.

Julianna got a wash rag, turned on the faucet, and let the warm water soak through the soft terry cloth. She put it on her face and felt the water trickle down her neck onto her fuzzy pink robe. She reached for the burgundy hand towel hanging next to the sink and dried her face, then stared at her reflection in the mirror. She was pale, mascara smudged under her eyes.

"Just a minute," she responded.

Her mind raced wildly. *How can this be how can they both be here? Okay*, she thought, *calm down. There has to be a rational explanation.*

She cleaned herself up, took off the mascara with cold cream, and brushed her hair and teeth. She looked at the bandage wrapped tightly around the top of her head.

Okay I can do this, she thought as she walked back sheepishly to the bedroom.

Anya and Dr. Swensen looked at her with concern as she pulled back the covers and crawled into bed.

"Hello, Julianna," he said in a thick Swedish accent. "I'm sorry we're meeting under these circumstances, but when Anya told me how concerned she was about you, I offered my services."

Even though his accent was prevalent, his English was very good. Julianna just stared at him, unable to respond. She was in disbelief. He was Dr. Briggs from her dream...or nightmare. It all seemed so real.

He walked over to her. His gray hair was thinning on top, and his neatly trimmed beard was a thick salt and pepper color. He had a kind face with piercing blue eyes. Prominent crow's feet lined his tanned face when he smiled.

"Do you mind?" he asked, and he reached for a pen light from the pocket of his gray flannel suit and checked her eyes.

"They seem to be properly dilated" he murmured.

About that time, Eric walked into the room with glasses of lemonade on a tray and set it down on the nightstand beside the bed.

"Maybe you should look at the knot on her head," Eric whispered to Doctor Swensen.

Doctor Swensen asked Julianna to sit on the rocking chair. He put on surgical gloves and started unwrapping the bandage she felt a tingling sensation, the wound got very warm. He stood looking at the back of Julianna's head, peering through the dried blood that had soaked through her hair.

"That's remarkable," he stammered.

"What?" questioned Eric, and both Anya and Eric went to look at Julianna's wound.

"It's healed," Doctor Swensen said, seemingly astounded, "but not just healed, it's like it never happened."

Doctor Swensen and Anya just looked at each other.

"But last night I changed the bandage myself and there was a huge gash and a knot," Eric stammered.

"See for yourself." Doctor Swensen motioned.

Eric probed through her hair trying to find the wound, then looked at the Doctor and Anya in amazement. Julianna felt her head. What had recently been gut wrenching pain was gone. There was no bump, no scab, nothing.

"I've never seen anything like this before... I've read about it in medical journals about plants and insects, but not mammals. I need to run some tests on you," Doctor Swensen said.

"No, no, that's quite alright," Julianna replied. "I just want this to be over with. I want to get back to work on my research. I've already lost a couple of days, and I have deadlines to meet."

She looked at them and shrugged her shoulder. Her mind was made up.

Chapter 5

THE next day Julianna once again walked up the cobble-stone stairway to the library. She was startled by the shrill cries of the crows. She looked up at the roof line of the historic brick building and saw black silhouettes of crows perched high above on the eaves of the ominous building. She could feel their beady eyes staring down at her. She could almost imagine their disappointment the day of her accident that they didn't have the chance to pick her bones clean.

Evil Vultures, she thought as she entered through the glass doors into the library's marble slated foyer.

She had always loved libraries, but this one was different. It was cold and dank, and it smelled different than the library back home in Boston. It smelled of disinfectant and moth balls. As she stepped up the marble stairs into the library's office, she saw the librarian spraying a cleaner on the counters. The librarian quickly looked up as Julianna stepped up to the counter.

"It's you," she gasped as she put the rag down and walked towards Julianna. She just stared at Julianna then cocked her head and asked, "How are you feeling?"

Even though the words of the Librarian seemed kind, they didn't match her demeanor. She still seemed cold without any emotion.

She's probably just relieved I didn't sue, Julianna thought to herself.

"I'm fine," Julianna stated matter-of-factly. "The reason I'm back is the news clipping you copied for me the other day…the day of my accident, well it was the wrong one. The picture was different. I think you copied the wrong one."

"There was only one picture" the librarian said coolly.

"Well could I please have the micro film?"

"I believe they're still here." The librarian searched through the drawers and pulled out the cartridge with the micro film and handed it to Julianna. Then she turned her back and started cleaning again.

Julianna walked back to the archives and sat in front of an ancient micro film viewer. She scanned through the news articles, but was unable to find the picture with Emily's face. Only her back was showing.

"That's so strange," she thought out loud.

"What's so strange," a voice from behind her questioned.

Julianna turned and smiled.

"I'm glad to see you're okay. I'm sorry I wasn't here to help you after your accident, but I was out of town on a book tour."

"Oh I'm fine now. What are you doing here?" Julianna asked.

"Same as you I suspect," replied Lauren in her thick British accent. "Trying to gen up."

"You're researching the Ericksons?" Julianna asked.

"Oh no…Blimey, who are they? No, I'm writing a book on the Salem witch trials." She saw the look of uneasiness on Julianna's face. "I know. How macabre, right?"

"Yeah." Julianna raised her eyebrows and nodded.

Lauren continued to explain about the history behind it.

"Do you know the Newlington Estate was one of the original sites where they actually burned the witches? There's a plaque dedicated to it behind the rose garden--where they tied them to stakes and torched them. And they have honest-to-God dungeons in the basement of that mansion."

Julianna's eyes got big. "Eric's trying to sell that estate to Anya. I wonder if she knows." Julianna gasped.

"She abso-bloody-lootly does... She's the one who told me," Lauren replied.

"I wonder if Eric knows," Julianna pondered, "and if he does why he never told me."

Just then her cell phone vibrated in her coat pocket. It was Eric.

"Speak of the devil," Julianna laughed. "Hi sweetie, what's up?"

Eric wanted her to meet him at the Newlington Estate. She was excited to see it and especially to ask him if he was aware of its torrid past. She asked Lauren if she could return the micro film and carefully held on to the rail as she went down the cobblestone steps to her yellow Volkswagen bug. She was very proud of her new car. She had purchased it entirely on her own with the commission money she had gotten from her last two children's books. She opened the car door and smelled the new car smell of leather and lilacs which Eric had picked and put in the vase on the dashboard.

She scooted into the warm black leather seat, shut the door, and opened her sunroof. The Newlington Estate wasn't far from town. The sun was just creeping out from behind a cloud, and it shone brightly. It was mid-summer and all the flowers were in full bloom. As she drove she noticed the rolling green pastures dotted with cows leisurely munching on lush green grass. Further down the road she noticed dark clouds looming ahead and quickly reached up and closed the sunroof.

It started pouring, and her windshield wipers could barely keep up. She grasped the wheel and tried to see through the downpour. Then the rain suddenly stopped. In the distance she saw something black in the road. It looked like some kind of animal. As she got closer, she thought maybe just a black garbage bag. Suddenly it moved. She jumped, slammed on her brakes, and skidded to a stop. What she'd thought was a garbage bag was a young girl shrouded in black. The girl jumped up and looked at Julianna. Her face was coated with black soot. Her hair was a stringy, dirty brown. She looked terrified and ran into the nearby forest and disappeared. Julianna just sat stunned in her car, not knowing whether to be terrified or to go after the young girl.

Her cell phone rang and she jumped. It was Eric.

"Where are you?" he asked.

"I'm almost there. Oh my God, you can't believe what just happened. There was a girl in the middle of the road, and she ran into the woods terrified."

"Uh huh, when do you think you can be here? I need to take this call." The phone went dead.

Julianna hung up the phone and threw it in her purse. Ever since her accident he'd been acting differently towards her.

"He thinks I'm looney because of my concussion," she sighed.

Julianna drove up to the mansion. She gasped; it took her breathe away. The architecture was exquisite, made up of large gray masonry blocks with ivy climbing up the walls. Wisteria blossomed over the archway to the enormous copper and bronze etched doorway. Gargoyles mounted on the edge of the gables looked like they were ready to pounce on uninvited visitors. The sun hit the door, blinding her. When she turned her head, she saw Eric's parked SUV under a tree. He was still talking on his cell.

Eric had told her that there were fifty plus acres of beautifully manicured lawns, rose gardens, tennis courts, swimming pools, golf course and an abundance of sculptures and fountains and to top it off a airstrip with a large hanger. She could hardly wrap her mind around the elaborate wealth. Eric had explained that the 15,000 square foot interior had been renovated, keeping the same architectural heritage. She couldn't wait to go inside.

She drove up beside him, and he quickly hung up and opened the door for her.

"Oh how debonair, sir," she laughingly teased.

"Well, how do you like it?" he said, grinning.

Her irritation towards him dissipated and her heart melted as she gazed at her handsome husband.

"It's so beautiful," Julianna sighed.

"It's even better inside. Come on." He grabbed her hand and unlocked the enormous door.

The grandeur of the foyer was breathtaking. It was as big as their apartment. White marble floors with two stairways led up to the second floor. The railings were gold plated with rosewood inlays that gleamed as the sun blazed through the large etched windows. Two huge chandeliers with teardrop crystals were on either side of the room. There was a large, marble life-sized sculpture of an angel reaching up to the heavens, his wings unfurled. In the middle of the foyer was a round cherry wood table with an enormous vase filled with a beautiful bouquet of roses lilacs lilies and babies breath. To the right was an entrance leading to an office. She saw a huge built-in desk with burgundy leather furnishings, a granite fireplace, and oriental rugs. To the left, through French doors, was a library with floor-to-ceiling mahogany book cases, with ladders that slid along the length of them. The shelves were full of manuscripts and first editions.

Velvet furnishings in pale seafoam were in this room along with a green marble fireplace with a gilded gold screen covered with cupids. Above the fireplace was an authentic Michelangelo painting. Eric had told her about it before, and she walked closer to view the beautiful painting of Angels looking down from the heavens on suffering souls on Earth. It took her breathe away. On the mantel was an ornate gold and metal box. It had cherubs and Angels covering it. Her finger-tips felt the intricate details, and then electricity jolted her hand.

She jumped backwards, and turned around to tell Eric. People were surrounding her. They were everywhere, dressed in ball gowns and suits. She looked down at her clothes. She was wearing a pale green satin gown with long white gloves. She was terrified and ran into the next room to see a group of girls huddled together whispering. A young girl about sixteen years old in a baby blue satin dress turned around, her emerald green eyes transfixed on Julianna. It was exactly like in the news clipping; it was Emily Erickson.

Julianna came out of her trance as if she'd been pushed and fell to the floor. Eric ran over to her and helped her up. "Are you alright?"

"Yeah…I'm fine," she lied.

She couldn't tell him. She couldn't tell anyone. They'd think she was crazy.

"I just tripped over the rug," she said, brushing her clothes off.

"This is the ball room... How many houses have a ball-room?" he laughed. "Watch this." He pushed a button on the wall, and the windows went black. A gigantic screen came down on the far side of the room. He pressed another button and sections of the floor lifted up and plush theater seats rose from the floor. "Now it's a theater. Isn't this great?"

His exuberance would have been contagious, but Julianna was still reeling from her vision. She had to find out why this was happening to her.

Eric continued showing her the mansion's many beautiful rooms and the surrounding grounds. Then they came to a rose garden.

"Eric did you know that during the Salem witch trial, they killed innocent people here?"

Eric's exuberance quickly turned to stoic silence, and he stared at her.

"I did hear something," he said coolly. "You can't believe every old wives' tale you hear."

"Well, I don't, but this is true. Lauren is doing research on it and--"

"Shh," Eric snapped. "Something like this might stop the sale."

"Eric, Anya is the one who told Lauren about it."

"About what?"

Eric and Julianna spun around to see Anya and her entourage walking towards them.

"About innocent people being burned at the stake as witches," Julianna responded.

"Yes, isn't it fascinating?" Anya's eyes glistened with amusement. "And I do believe they did their dastardly deeds right behind these hedges."

As she pointed, one of her many assistants parted the hedge and beckoned them through to the other side. It was as if they were in another world, as if the smoke still hadn't cleared from centuries before. They only walked a little way in to the thicket, and the brambles and prickly thorns dug into their clothing. It seemed to Julianna as if the foliage had come to life, pulling them relentlessly deeper into its evil.

"Julianna! Julianna, are you okay," Eric asked as Julianna came out of her trance and they made their way back to the rose garden.

She was shaken, but she didn't dare tell him what had happened.

"I need to have that cleared and excavated," Anya exclaimed as she brushed off her clothes. "I'm sure we'll be able to find artifacts. Wouldn't that be fascinating!"

"Yeah, I guess," Julianna said, still shaken, as she looked at Eric's astonished expression.

"You do know that's the reason I'm buying this place," Anya said, staring at Eric.

He shrugged. "Uh huh," he muttered.

"Actually," she went on. "My studio is planning to do a film on the Salem witch trials. That's why I came here, and when I saw this marvelous mansion and found out its torrid past... Well, I couldn't resist," Anya giggled.

"Eric do you have the papers?" Anya asked.

"Yeah," Eric muttered, still reeling from Anya's admission of the mansion's horrendous history.

After the papers were signed and Anya's attorney looked them over, everyone celebrated the sale with champagne on the credenza. Before they had finished the first glass, the moving vans arrived with scores of workers unloading the huge sets with cranes and forklifts.

Julianna and Eric thanked Anya and left to go have a romantic celebration of their own.

Chapter 6

THE next day with somewhat of a hangover they started talking about buying a house with Eric's commission. Julianna viewed some houses online.

"You won't believe this," Julianna exclaimed. "The people I'm researching for my book have relatives still living here, and they're selling their house."

"It must be a new listing. How much?" Eric asked.

"Oh the bargain price is fifteen million," Julianna laughed.

"A bit out of our league, don't you think?" Eric replied.

"Yeah, maybe," Julianna chuckled as she nibbled some dry wheat toast and popped some aspirin into her mouth, gulping it down with tomato juice. "Oh, remind me never to drink that much champagne ever, ever again." She put her head in her hands. "Maybe if my headache goes away, we could go and take a look at it. You know it would help with my research--kill two birds with one stone."

"Yeah, I guess," Eric responded in between gargling from the bathroom.

"Okay, let me take a hot shower, and maybe I'll start feeling better." She trudged off to the upstairs bathroom.

Eric contacted the Ericksons and set up a meeting for later on that day. As they drove through the hills, up the winding driveway to the estate, they marveled at the magnificent view.

The Ericksons' mansion wasn't nearly as grand as the Newlington Estate, but this was homier. It was much smaller--12,000 square feet and twenty acres of land. The view was exquisite--rolling green pastures and a large lake. The veranda offered gorgeous views of mountains and sunrises, at least according to the listing.

Julianna thoroughly enjoyed meeting the Ericksons. It was just them living in their beautiful mansion, along with twenty-five servants, cooks, and gardeners. They were in their seventies, still vibrant and healthy. Mr. Erickson was a tall, thin, distinguished-looking man with a full head of silver-grey hair. He was tan with a ruggedly handsome face. His wife was petite with shoulder length dark hair and a porcelain complexion with hardly any wrinkles except a little crow's feet around her eyes. Julianna liked that about her because it meant she had a good sense of humor and smiled all the time.

Julianna noticed pictures around the living room. In them the Ericksons were years younger, seated with three beautiful children, two boys and a girl. They had a handsome family.

"They're all grown up and moved away," Mrs. Erickson sighed.

They went out on the veranda and drank lemonade. Julianna told them about her research on their ancestors, over two hundred years ago. They were very interested and offered her access to old diaries and their family trees. Julianna was ecstatic.

"But please do come here to do your research in the family library," Mrs. Erickson insisted.

"Oh, yes, of course," Julianna happily agreed.

They went on an extensive tour of the house. When they

came to the third floor, Julianna started feeling strange. Her dream came back to her, and then she entered that very room.

"This room hasn't been used much. My children didn't like coming up here. They were afraid, said they heard things at night." Mrs. Erickson laughed. "I never heard anything. Did you dear?"

Mr. Erickson just chuckled and shook his head. Eric laughed too, but Julianna felt the hair raise up on the back of her neck as she recognized the layout of the room. She walked over to the same vanity she saw in her dream and stared at her reflection in the mirror.

Maybe I am going crazy, she thought.

Eric and Julianna said their goodbyes to the Ericksons.

"Do come back soon," Mrs. Erickson said, giving them both a big hug.

"Okay, we will, thanks," Julianna responded.

As they drove away, Julianna was sad, as if she was leaving her long lost family. She felt an instant connection to them. She looked back at the grand house, her eyes traveling up the gleaming white and brick mansion to the third floor bedroom. For a brief moment, she swore she saw a silhouette of a small girl looking out the window, but then it was gone.

Quit imagining things, she thought to herself.

She turned and smiled at Eric. "Cool house," she said. He nodded.

The next two days went by quickly as the sale of the Newlington Estate went through. Eric and Julianna celebrated by looking for a starter home. They found a quaint brownstone on a great tree-lined cul-de-sac, which was on the outskirts of town near the Ericksons' estate.

"I can't believe how beautiful this house is," Julianna sighed.

Eric chuckled. "Yeah, it's just the right size, too…but the yard." He looked at the brown grass and dead shrubs. "It needs so much work."

That's what commission checks are for," Julianna laughed teasingly. Eric grinned.

While waiting for their house to close, Julianna dove into her research. Between visiting the Ericksons and the Langendorf Library, she was swamped with sifting through old family diaries and letters, but never able to find anything about the sisters. It was like they never existed, except in the one news clipping she'd found earlier.

Mrs. Erickson gave Julianna permission to look around in the attic. "We're supposed to have a storm, the weather report says," Mrs. Erickson sighed as she showed Julianna the stairway up to the attic. "I'll be along shortly. I need to take my medicine."

As Julianna ascended the dark stairway, she switched on the light, but it soon flickered and went out. She heard the wind outside begin to blow, banging the shutters methodically against the house. It was four o'clock, but the beautiful summer day disappeared as black clouds loomed over the sun. The sky was black, and Julianna could barely see. Julianna finally made it up to the attic. She walked into the dusty room filled with old chests, rocking chairs, and various dolls and antiques. Then she looked out the window.

She was five stories up. She saw the lake, the trees blowing almost sideways. She was astonished as she watched a funnel rise out of the lake and make a path of destruction as it headed toward the mansion.

Mrs. Erickson yelled up the stairs, "A tornado is coming! You need to come down to the cellar."

Terrified, Julianna grabbed the stair railing and felt each footstep slowly going down. When she reached the door, it slammed shut. She turned the doorknob to no avail; it wouldn't open. She screamed for Mrs. Erickson, but the wind sounded like a freight train. She could barely hear her own voice. The entire house shook and groaned. Julianna fell against the wall and crumpled to the floor. The windows shattered and the wind whipped through the attic. Papers and furniture flew, crashing above her. She put her hands over her head and crouched down against the stairwell, her back pressed up against the door.

The storm suddenly stopped as fast as it had started. Julianna's heart was beating so hard she could hear the pounding in her head. She stood up and brushed the glass and debris out of her hair and clothes. The door clicked open, and she slowly opened it and went into the hallway. The lights in the hall flickered as she walked towards the stairway. Her fingertips slid against the wainscoting, then she grabbed the railing and started down the stairs.

As she walked down to the third floor, she was strangely compelled to go to the bedroom that she'd seen in her dream. Hesitantly, she walked towards the door. She heard whispering. She peered through the key hole and saw the back of a little girl crying. A women was consoling her. The little girl was dressed in an old fashioned black dress. She was sitting on the bed. The woman wore an apron over a grey dress. She looked like a maid. The little girl whispered to the woman as Julianna crouched outside the door, trying to make out what they were saying.

"How could they do something like that?" the girl sobbed.

"There, there," the woman said as she stroked the little girl's long brown hair.

Suddenly the little girl turned and walked towards the door.

Julianna's blood ran cold. It was the same girl she'd seen in the road.

She bolted away from the keyhole, waiting for the door to open. Nothing happened. She crouched back down and looked again. An eye was staring back at her. She jumped back and screamed.

"Are you alright?" Mrs. Erickson asked as she walked up the stairs.

"Somebody's in there," Julianna pointed as she trembled, her back pressed tightly against the adjacent wall.

Mrs. Erickson opened the door. "Nobody's here," she said as she looked around the room. She turned and looked at Julianna. "Are you alright?" she asked again. This time she walked over and grabbed Julianna's hands.

Still trembling, Julianna walked in the room and looked around. The bedspread and furnishings were different from what she had seen before. She sat on the bed feeling light headed. Mrs. Erickson sat beside her, putting a motherly arm around her.

"I heard you scream," she said.

"I thought I saw something," Julianna whispered. "It must have been a shadow…I must have imagined it." She looked down at her fidgeting hands.

"Like I said before, my children heard things in this room. Just because I didn't doesn't mean I didn't believe them."

Julianna looked into her eyes as if to say thank you for validating what she was afraid to admit. She wasn't ready to tell her what had happened. Maybe she never would; she didn't want to jeopardize their friendship.

"Well, this house held up pretty well except for a few broken windows," Mrs. Erickson exclaimed.

"Some windows in the attic blew in too," Julianna replied. "I...I saw the tornado come out of the lake."

Mrs. Erickson nodded. "Well, I'll have to get Clarence and Ed up there right away to estimate the damage."

Just then Julianna's cell rang. It was Eric.

"Are you alright?" he stammered.

"Yeah, I'm fine. Are you?"

"Yeah, but I have some bad news." His voice sounded defeated.

"What's wrong?" She was afraid of his response.

"Our Brownstone is gone... It's totally destroyed!"

"Oh no, you've got to be kidding." Tears started streaming down her face.

All Mrs. Erickson could do was sit and watch Julianna as she paced back and forth.

"Eric did we have insurance?"

"Yeah we did, fortunately. Honey everything's going to be okay, except our lease on our apartment is up in a week. We need to find a place to stay."

"Well, that's just perfect," she said sarcastically. "Okay honey I'll talk to you soon. Love you, Eric."

"Love you, too. Bye."

They both hung up, and Julianna threw her phone on the bed, just missing Mrs. Erickson.

"Oh, sorry," she said, and she started sobbing and explained about their brownstone.

Mrs. Erickson handed a tissue to her and offered a suggestion. "Why don't you and Eric move in here while you look for another place. I know it'll be alright with Charles, and we'd love the company. We've come to think of you both as family."

Julianna's tears stopped as she dabbed them from her eyes, and a huge smile spread across her face.

"Really… you'd do that?"

"Well of course. There are plenty of rooms," Mrs. Erickson laughingly replied.

"Okay, that's so nice of you!" Julianna jumped off the bed, then looked at Mrs. Erickson solemnly.

"Could we stay somewhere besides the third floor?"

Mrs. Erickson saw the look of fear in Julianna's eyes. "Sure, Julianna. You know you can tell me anything, and it'll be okay."

Julianna just stood there weighing her options. Knowing how her children felt about the third floor, maybe it would be okay.

"Okay, but can we please go downstairs. This place gives me the creeps!"

"Sure," Mrs Erickson said, nodding her head.

Chapter 7

A S they sat at the kitchen table, the sun streamed in through the windows. The weather outside was beautiful once again, as if nothing had happened. Sitting on the quaint walnut table, a handmade doily rested in the center with a bowl of assorted fruit. It made Julianna feel at home, a home she really never had growing up. Her mother had died when she was just a baby and her father, an archeologist, was gone most of the time out of the country on digs, leaving her usually with her mom's sister, Aunt Linda. Although she was very nice, she was a divorced socialite with her own agenda, often leaving Julianna with the nanny Ms. Isabelle who was very strict.

"Julianna, would you like some fruit?"

"Oh yes, thank you Mrs. Erickson."

"You know, lets not be so formal. Please call me Charlotte," she gently said patting Julianna's hand from across the table.

Julianna nodded, grinning, grabbed a handful of large grapes and popped one in her mouth. She felt the crunch of delicious grape juice explode in her mouth.

"These are really good."

"Homegrown." Charlotte grinned, grabbed some herself and started eating them as Nellie the cook served them coffee and sugar cookies. The house was bustling with activity as handymen and maids cleaned up broken glass and replaced windows.

"Well, are you going to tell me what happened up there?" Charlotte asked.

"Okay, but please…I don't want you to think I'm a nut case. Actually, a lot of things have happened."

Julianna swallowed hard. Knowing the history about Charlotte's children and the fear that they'd had, she felt she had to tell. When she finished telling Charlotte about the woman and the little girl and seeing the same girl on the road, Charlotte didn't seem surprised at all.

"I've heard this before," Charlotte sighed.

"From who?" Julianna asked.

"My children--all of them said they saw the very same thing you did. I can't explain it. Charles and I never saw or heard a thing, but they did and wouldn't go up there ever again."

Julianna finally had the courage to tell Charlotte about everything she'd experienced: the library, her accident, her dream about the Erickson sisters and about being in the third floor bedroom. She even told Charlotte about her weird experience at the Newlington Estate and the ballroom.

"Oh, that is strange," Charlotte commented. "You know, I'm going to tell you something. You said the only thing you couldn't find was more information about the sisters. Well, I might have some information. It's hearsay passed down from generation to generation, but I need to share it with you. About two hundred years ago people believed in witches, even though the Salem witch trials were dubbed unfair a century prior. Still, people were very superstitious and believed witches still existed and were kidnapping and killing children…putting evil spells on the people of Salem. Even the Salem witch trials where people were tortured into saying that their friends and relatives were witches, Secret Societies of vigilant groups existed. They would find religious cults that they deemed evil and kill them. They were horrible, horrible people." She dabbed her eyes with a hankie. "The very ones that accused them were the evil ones."

"Ms. Charlotte, why do you do this to yourself?" Nellie said to her in her thick southern drawl, rubbing Charlotte's back, trying to console her.

"I'm fine Nellie really, Julianna needs to know this for her research."

Charlotte regained her composure and went on. "The evil ones--the true devil worshipers--were drawing attention away from themselves by accusing the innocents. Then there were the children. They simply disappeared, dozens of them never to be seen again. Families were frantic. That's why some went on killing rampages. Then it suddenly stopped more than two hundred years ago. The children stopped disappearing. Everything went back to normal. Nobody knows how or why; they just felt the evil was gone. But that brings me to the debutante ball. It seems everything happened around the same time. The Erickson sisters--the story is they were best friends besides being sisters, until the love triangle. They both fell in love with the same man, but he only loved one of them. I don't know which one. Anyway, a wedding was planned. The other sister was desperate and went to a Wiccan, a women who lived in the woods, right around here in an old shack. She healed people and was a midwife, but she also made love potions. The sister paid her handsomely for a love potion and spiked the man's drink one night when having dinner at their parents house. The love potion worked and the engagement was called off. The betrayed sister was inconsolable, and it was said she tried to commit suicide by throwing herself down a flight of stairs... She almost died. That's really all I know. I don't know who was who. All I know is it was Emily and Victoria Erickson."

Julianna gasped. "That's the vision I had in my dream. It must have been Victoria who was betrayed. I was Victoria... How is that possible?"

"I don't know," Charlotte said, "but you had no idea about this story when you experienced that vision."

"My friend Lauren is doing research on the witches of Salem. I need to talk to her and see if she has any more information."

Chapter 8

JULIANNA thanked Charlotte and left the Ericksons. The tornado had touched down and made a straight line from the Ericksons' lake to the mansion, then to her brownstone, leaving a wake of destruction, turned over cars, broken trees and downed power lines. She was amazed the Ericksons had electricity at all until she found out later they had an emergency generator.

Julianna called Lauren and made arrangements to meet her at the local coffee shop by Eric's office.

"I'd like a tall, double shot, skinny, vanilla latte," Lauren ordered.

"Make that two," Julianna piped in.

The sun had come out, and it was 85 degrees.

"Boy, this weather's wonky. One minute a tornado, the next this." Lauren gestured up to the blue sky.

"I know. How's your apartment? Anything happen?" Julianna asked.

"Oh no, it's the bee's knees. The tornado missed it completely," Lauren said. "How about you?"

Julianna just shook her head.

"Blimey, Jules! What happened? Can it be fixed?"

"No, total loss," Julianna sighed, "but we were totally covered by insurance."

"Bloody hell. Well, at least that's a relief, but I bet you're gutted!" Lauren said, blowing on the hot coffee.

As they walked outside, they realized no tables were available. The park was across the street, and some empty picnic tables sat in the shade of majestic oak trees.

"It's bloody hot out here." Lauren took her sweater off, tied the sleeves around her waist, and sat down in the shade. "Have you seen your brownstone?" she inquired.

"Not yet... I don't think there's anything to see. We're going to go with the insurance adjustor later today," Julianna sadly stated. "The good thing is the Ericksons offered to let us stay with them until we find something else."

"Wicked! That's so nice," Lauren exclaimed.

Julianna nodded. "They're really great! But, anyway, I need your help. Have you found out any information about the Erickson sisters, Victoria and Emily?"

"There was a tad about a debutante ball and a fire that nearly destroyed the Newlington Estate, but that's about it," Lauren said. "Maybe if I google their names, I'll find out some more info."

Lauren put her laptop on the picnic table and typed in the information. A bird dropping fell onto her keypad, then on her head.

"Oh gross," she exclaimed and looked up to see hundreds of crows perched in the oak trees above them. "Bloody birds!" Lauren yelled, wiping the droppings out of her hair with a napkin. "Sod off!"

They started cawing. It was deafening. Then one flew down and knocked the laptop off the picnic table, another dove down and gashed Lauren's forehead.

"Lauren, we've got to get out of here," Julianna screamed as the crows dove down on them.

Lauren was knocked down and fell onto her laptop, smashing it, while crows attacked her relentlessly, pecking at her as she screamed, covering her head. Julianna tried to help Lauren, but the crows also knocked her down, covering both of them like black tarps. The screams startled the customers at the coffee shop, and they ran over to fight off the vicious crow attack. Eric heard the commotion and came out of his office to see the crowd at the park fighting off the crows, not realizing it was Julianna and Lauren. It was pandemonium with people swinging rolled up papers and purses at the vicious birds. Soon the attack ended, leaving dozens of people with deep gashes and abrasions. Lauren was unconscious, and Julianna knelt beside her sobbing.

Eric ran over to them. "Oh my God. Are you okay?"

"Yeah, I'm fine," Julianna answered through tears, "it was just like before, Eric. The crows--they don't want us to know."

Eric's puzzled expression just frustrated Julianna more. The ambulance sirens loomed closer, and soon EMT's were putting Lauren on a stretcher. A fire engine arrived, and firemen helped victims across the street to the coffee shop to check their vital signs.

"Miss, are you alright?" an EMT asked.

Julianna looked at Eric, then the young man. "Yes, I'm fine" she answered.

Oddly, she hardly had any wounds at all, just a few scratches. Eric and Julianna looked up at the trees. There were no signs of crows at all, only a couple of robins flying overhead.

"Where did they go?" Julianna asked, looking at Eric.

Chapter 9

THAT night on T.V., the weird crow attack made the national news. And strangely it was happening all over the country. One man was actually killed in Ohio. Witnesses said he was on his tractor, and the crows attacked him, knocking him off before the tractor ran over him. Then the crows would just mysteriously disappear.

"My God, what's happening," Eric gasped as he set his coffee down on the table.

"I don't know," Julianna responded, terror in her eyes. "We need to visit Lauren. She doesn't have any family here."

Julianna called the hospital to see how she was doing, but her cell kept going to voice mail, so Eric and Julianna drove to Salem Memorial. There were dozens of T.V. crews from everywhere outside the hospital trying to interview people about the crow attack. Eric and Julianna made their way through the barrage of people being questioned by reporters. They found out Lauren's room number and headed there. Anya and her entourage came out, just as Eric and Julianna rounded the corner.

"We've got to quit meeting like this," Anya teased, smiling at Eric and not noticing Julianna at all.

Anya's weird outlook on life really was starting to irritate her. Anya didn't seem to care that there had been a crow attack or that people had been hurt and killed. No, it was just more exciting drama for her to draw from for her movie. The fact that her new home was the site of ancient murders and macabre rituals excited her. She relished in the very fact that chaos was running rampant in the town of Salem.

Just as she was about to voice her opinion to Anya, Eric interrupted. It was as if he'd read her mind and saved her from making a huge mistake. "So Anya, when does production start?"

"Tomorrow," Anya giggled.

Julianna felt her blood start to boil.

Doesn't she care about anything but her stupid movie and career, she thought.

Just then Anya moved closer to Eric and grasped his hand. "I'm just glad to see you're okay with all the tornadoes and those terrible bird attacks. She brushed his hair from his forehead and suddenly turned towards Julianna. "You take care of this one. He's my favorite realtor."

Then she smiled at him a seductive smile, looked him up and down and smacked him on the butt as she walked away, her entourage following close behind her. Julianna was seething as Eric just turned red and looked at her with a sheepish grin.

Julianna and Eric entered Lauren's room; she was sitting up in bed on the phone. Seeing her like this made the last few annoying minutes melt away. Julianna was so happy to see her awake, vibrant, and laughing.

Lauren was on the phone. "*No*, Mum you don't need to come here. I'm fine, honestly…It was just a wonky, weird thing that happened…Really? Everywhere?"

She looked up, saw Eric and Julianna, and waved.

"No, Mum, really, I'm brilliant…wicked, Mum." She smiled again and made the talking hand puppet sign. "Mum, can I give you a bell later? I have some more visitors. Okay, Mum, love you, too... Bye, yeah, bye bye."

"Blimey," she sighed as she hung up the hospital phone. "I'm so glad to see you guys."

Julianna hugged her. Eric still looked embarrassed from Anya's advances, and Lauren noticed.

"Eric are you okay?"

Eric blushed. Lauren looked at Julianna, questioning.

"Oh, he'll be okay... He's just embarrassed because Anya was flirting with him right in front of me."

Lauren laughed. "Well it's not every day that a fit, glamorous actress tries to chat you up," Lauren teased.

Julianna started giggling too. Eric's face was now bright red.

"Come on, knock it off." Then he turn to Julianna and grasped her hands. "I hope you know nothing is going on. She's just getting weirder. I know she's my client but the deal is done. She needs to back off."

He was serious. This was really bugging him. Julianna could see it on his face.

"I'm going to steer clear of her." He sat down on the chair adjacent from Lauren's hospital bed.

"Okay honey" Julianna responded as she rubbed his shoulders. "I believe you." She kissed the top of his head.

Lauren sat up in her hospital bed. She had scratches all over her face and a patch over her left eye; both hands were wrapped in gauze, and she had a huge bandage on her forehead. "The telly said this has been happening all over the country?"

"Yeah," Julianna nodded. "Scientists don't know what to make of it; they've never seen the migration of crows this large before. It's tripled. And their behavior is crazy. At first scientists thought maybe the pesticides were making them act erratic, but the other birds are normal. They just don't have any answers."

Lauren listened intently. "Julianna, would you and Eric please go and buy me another laptop? I still need to do research and mine's gutted."

She reached for her purse, got her wallet out, and handed her debit card to Julianna.

"No, No we'll buy it for you," Julianna objected.

"Oh, blimey. No I couldn't ask you--" Lauren was stopped as Julianna put her hand gently over her mouth.

"Please, we want to," Julianna said.

"Ace," Lauren smiled. "Well then, I insist on helping you with your research." "Why do you think I'm doing this?" Julianna laughed. "We'll be back soon."

They hugged Lauren and left to go to the computer store in downtown Salem.

After purchasing the laptop, Eric glanced at his watch.

"Oh, crap. I forgot we're supposed to meet the insurance adjustor at the brownstone."

They hurried to the SUV and drove down the highway towards their brownstone. The trees that had lined the road to their cul-de-sac were no longer there. Instead they lay like match sticks lining the road, while PUD and city workers busily tried to clean the fallen trees and branches off the street. Some trees were still in the middle of the road, so they had to get out and walk. Still a few blocks from their home, they noticed most all the houses were intact, but when they got to their house, all that was left was the fireplace. It was a total loss. Bricks were everywhere. Julianna broke down sobbing as Eric wrapped his arms around her.

The inspector Mr. Pattison walked up and handed a Kleenex to Julianna. She gratefully accepted it.

"Wow, this took a direct hit, but luckily for you, you have optimum coverage and better yet, you hadn't moved in. There will be no problem getting you the full amount and then you can rebuild. But it will still be a couple of weeks for the paper work." He adjusted his glasses and started filling out paperwork on his clipboard.

"Eric, I forgot to tell you the Ericksons said we can stay with them till we find something else. We can even store our belongings in their barn."

"What a relief. We only have a week left at our apartment," Eric sighed.

"I hate moving."

"Mr. and Mrs. Hawthorn, will you please sign here?" Mr. Pattison asked.

"Sure," Eric replied, and they both signed.

"Sorry again about this," Mr. Pattison sighed. "Mother nature. Nothing you can do about it."

They shook hands, and he walked off, leaving them standing there amongst the rubble. Julianna noticed something was gleaming; a glare in the corner of her eye drew her attention to some rubble by the fireplace. She bent down and removed the rubble. It was the box from the mansion. She carefully picked it up with her sweater covering her hands.

"Why is this here?"

She looked at Eric, who shrugged and looked as bewildered as she felt.

Chapter 10

AS they drove back to the hospital, Julianna carefully examined the box. It was both gold and silver metal, about eight inches long and six inches wide. It stood about four inches high. There was no up or down to it. Small cherubs and angels were inlaid in a sort of rose gold. Some were upside down, some vertical, and some perpendicular, but all were different types of angels. Tiny stones--black obsidian is what they looked like--were laid on the circumference of each angle. There was no seam or hinges, no way to open it, and through her sweater, it felt warm. The box was almost pulsing or purring like a cat. This should have scared Julianna, but oddly it didn't; it comforted her. Still, she didn't want to touch it with her bare hands.

"Eric feel this."

He touched it through her sweater. It stopped.

"What?' he asked.

As soon as he removed his hand, it started again.

"It's purring!"

"Sure it is," he said, grinning at her.

"No, it's like a cat, but when you touched it, it stopped."

He laughed.

"Eric, I'm not kidding," she said glaring at him.

Eric just kept driving with a grin on his face. "Could this day get any weirder?" he sighed.

As they drove into the parking structure at the hospital, Julianna gently placed the box with her sweater wrapped around it into her purse while Eric carried the laptop in.

"I don't think they want you to have laptops in here," Eric warned.

They were right, but when they got into Lauren's room, she had already sneaked in and used her cell phone to google Emily and Victoria Erickson.

"It referred me to witches and Wiccans of Salem," she whispered as a nurse walked out of her room.

Lauren quickly took her cell out from under the covers and read: "In the late 1700's, there was a debutante ball that almost burnt the Newlington Estate down. The back east wing was destroyed, and there were several casualties. But it doesn't say who...Dodgy!" Lauren muttered.

"Here's your laptop, except it has to stay in the box," said Eric.

"Yeah, I found that out after you left. Thanks anyway! We already knew that about the Ericksons; I wish we could find out a tad more," Lauren murmured.

"Well I did, from Mrs. Erickson, I mean, Charlotte." Julianna proceeded to tell them everything that she'd learned. Then she said, "I'm going to tell you what happened to me." She looked at their skeptical faces as she finished. "I know you must think I'm crazy, but honestly it happened, and Charlotte said her kids heard and saw what I did. We're still not staying on the third floor...I'm just saying."

"Yes, this day did just get weirder." Eric sighed, shaking his head.

Julianna took the box covered with her sweater out of her purse.

"Blimey, what's that?" Lauren inquired.

"It's the box with angels on it, the one I touched at the mansion."

"Bee's knees! Why do you have it?" Lauren asked, reaching for it.

"No, don't touch it with your bare hands," she insisted. "It was at the ruins of our brownstone."

She un-wrapped it carefully and set it on top of the covers on Lauren's lap.

"Remember, don't touch it."

"God, it's beautiful," Lauren exclaimed. "It's vibrating! What's in it? It doesn't open. I can't find a seam or hinge. That's so bloody weird. Take it."

Julianna carefully wrapped it back up and started to put it in her purse. As she opened her purse she saw a beautiful golden pouch.

"What's this?"

She replaced the box and lifted the pouch out. Inside was a stunning gold hair comb set with rubies, emeralds and diamonds. It was so beautiful, it took their breath away.

"But how did it get here? From the box?" Julianna questioned.

They just looked at each other.

"Wait a minute, I've seen this before," Julianna explained. "It was in the debutante picture. I think Emily Erickson was wearing it."

"Lauren, we have to go." Julianna carefully placed the box and the comb in her purse. "I'll call you if I find out anything else."

She and Eric both rushed out the door.

"I need to look at the debutante picture," Julianna explained as they drove back to their apartment.

Eric and Julianna walked up the stairs and noticed the door was ajar. When Eric and Julianna walked inside the apartment, it was in total shambles. Everything was askew; files and drawers were flung everywhere. Julianna sank to her knees, frantically searching for the pictures, but they were gone. Eric called 911 on his cell.

After the police left, Eric put his arm around Julianna and kissed her cheek. "It'll be alright. I need some coffee, want some?"

Julianna nodded her head. They sat down amongst the disarray and sipped their coffee.

"It looks like the only thing they were interested in was your research," Eric said as he rubbed his hand through his hair. "It's so weird. Why?"

"I'll tell you why. Because..." She was scared. "Because it's the answer to everything"

Just then the phone rang, and they both jumped. It was Lauren.

"You're not going to bloody believe this, but the box is called the 'Angel Box.' It was in the traveling exhibit at the museum in Salem from the Smithsonian. And, get this, it was donated years ago from descendants of the Ericksons."

Julianna gasped and dropped the phone.

"Honey, are you alright?" Eric stammered and grabbed the phone.

Lauren explained everything to Eric, and he told her about the break in and the missing research.

"But Eric, that's dodgy. How did it get on your property?" Lauren questioned.

No one had an answer.

The next day Eric and Julianna went to the library to get

more pictures. A perky blonde girl was behind the counter, and she greeted them cheerfully with a big smile.

"Howdy, may I help ya?"

Her accent sounded southern. She was a pleasant surprise from the other librarian.

"Yes, please. I was in here a couple weeks ago, and the other librarian helped me. Would you happen to know if I could talk to her."

The girl looked confused. "Y'all must be confused. I'm the only one here, with the budget cuts and all."

She looked at Julianna's bewildered face.

"I'm Mary Margaret, by the way."

She reached across the counter and shook both their hands.

"No, you don't understand. The other woman, she's older, has a bun, brown hair, glasses."

"No, nobody like that here. I've been here five years, and before me it was Gertrude, but she's African American, and she retired. I think she's in a nursing home now."

Julianna's head was spinning. "I was in here a week ago."

Mary Margaret piped in. "Oh, honey, we only reopened a couple days ago because of the renovation and all. Had to fix the dry rot."

What is going on? Julianna thought.

Eric piped in. "Could we please see some news clippings and micro film about a debutante ball in 1792 with the Erickson sisters?"

"Doesn't sound familiar," she said, "but all the information will be in the next room."

Julianna looked around. Strangely everything was so updated, so modern, nothing at all like it had been a week ago.

"Now exactly what do y'all want to see?" Mary Margaret asked as she sat down at the laptop.

"Erickson, Victoria and Emily. The debutante ball about two hundred years ago."

She quickly typed in the information. "Here it is, and I guess there's some micro film too, from the Salem Gazette."

She put on some surgical gloves and found the film, which she placed carefully in the viewer. Julianna and Eric viewed every picture. It showed the mansion and the damage from the fire, but the pictures she had seen before weren't there.

"Well that's it," Mary Margaret explained. "Can I help you with anything else?"

"No," Julianna stammered. "When did you remodel this place?"

"Oh, like I said, we just got back in here a couple days ago. The library was closed for about a month. Then, before that, the big remodel was about twenty years ago. There are pictures in the entryway showing the library through the years. Y'all might like to take a little looksee." She smiled.

Julianna's face went blank.

"Honey, are ya alright?"

"She's fine," Eric said, grabbing her hand and guiding her out to the entryway.

"What's going on? I feel like I'm going crazy."

They looked at the numerous photographs of the library's renovations throughout the years that lined the entry's hallway.

"Eric…Oh my God."

She pointed her shaking finger at a picture dated 1792. It was a librarian, brown hair pulled back in a severe bun. Her stare was cold and lifeless.

"She's the one who helped me."

Chapter 11

THE next day at the hospital, they sat and pondered their options.

"This is too bloody weird," Lauren exclaimed.

"I know, but you do believe me?" Julianna's eyes pleaded for some sign that they believed what she'd told them. "I showed you the pictures."

"I know," Lauren sighed.

"Did you--" Eric asked.

"Go to the library?" Lauren nodded. "But I never saw a mare with a bun. Actually, I didn't see anyone but Julianna."

"But you were there when it was suppose to be closed," he continued.

"Yeah, I guess." She looked at Julianna. "Don't worry. I don't think you're a nutter."

"Thank you," Julianna whispered. "What are we going to do about the box? They're going to think we stole it."

"Maybe they haven't discovered it's gone. It hasn't been on the news," Eric said as he leafed through the newspaper. "And besides, we didn't. It was at the mansion."

"Well, I kept researching. It's called the 'Angel Box.' I found out bits 'n bobs after you left last night...very dodgy information...mainly a weird legend."

"What?" they both questioned.

"Well, I couldn't find anything on the comb. I sort of buggered that up, but..." She paused, only making Eric and Julianna's curiosity overflow. "Okay, there is a legend, and it seems to be in every blooming religion."

Eric and Julianna were on the edge of their very uncomfortable hospital chairs.

Lauren continued. "It dates back to way before Christ. Okay, the story goes that when God threw his favorite Angel, aka Lucifer, out of Heaven, Lucifer nicked the angel box."

"What?" Eric didn't understand.

"Oh, sorry." Lauren turned red, realizing she should try to refrain from using her British jargon. "Stole it. Anyway, God condemned him to the underworld. He hit the ground with such force that it formed a crater and eventually the crater became a lake."

Eric laughed, but Julianna felt sick.

"So people think that it's evil because the devil had it." Julianna's stomach turned, remembering what happened when she touched it.

"Well the powers it possesses are suppose to be bloody unbelievable."

Julianna got up holding her stomach and began pacing.

"The Ericksons, Anya, and the museum are the last ones to possess it," she whispered.

They all looked at each other.

"We need to return it to the mansion," Eric said, and he found some disposable medical gloves by the sink to put on.

"Oh yeah, that's gonna protect you." Julianna squirmed.

"About as much as your sweater," Eric snapped back.

They started out the door.

"Wait, I wanna go," Lauren pleaded, and she hit the buzzer for the nurse.

Checking Lauren out took forever, and by the time she was released, the day had turned into a dark and dreary evening. As the SUV approached the mansion, it took on a different persona in the gloomy dusk. The immense ark of a building cast haunting shadows across the landscape.

"Scared?" Eric asked the girls.

"You have no idea," Lauren's voice quivered.

Julianna couldn't even talk. She was terrified. The mansion was dark.

"It doesn't look like anyone's here," Eric observed.

There were trailers, trucks, booms and scaffolding everywhere, getting the mansion ready for the upcoming movie. On the north side of the mansion, Eric parked the SUV under an oak tree.

"Okay, you guys stay here. I still have a key, and I'll go and put the box on the mantel."

"We're not staying here, Eric. If you think you're going alone, you are crazy," Julianna blurted out.

"We're going with you," Lauren piped in.

There was no changing their minds. The trio quietly got out of the SUV and gently shut the doors.

"Come on," Eric whispered.

They maneuvered like Navy Seals to the back door of the mansion, entering through the kitchen. Eric clicked the locked door open, and they carefully walked in, shutting the door behind them. It smelled like sweet incense from the flowers' aroma. The moon's glow bounced off the granite countertops, casting eerie shadows on the walls.

Julianna looked at Eric. "It was in the library next to the Michelangelo painting."

"They have a blooming Michelangelo?" Lauren gasped.

"Shh!" they both responded.

They quickly went to the library.

"Doesn't it seem daft that they don't have security here?" Lauren whispered.

Just then, alarms went off and security officers burst through the front doors.

"Hands in the air," a scruffy-haired officer screamed.

Julianna dropped her purse, and they all raised their arms over their heads. The guards began patting them down, and then one of them grabbed Julianna's purse.

"No, please don't."

He just eyed her and proceeded to dump the contents on the floor.

Anya came running through the door. "What on earth is going on?"

"We found these perpetrators trying to steal part of the set," the guard explained.

"No, no, Anya we can explain," Eric interrupted.

She eyed them up and down. "Well you'd better do it quickly. The police are on their way."

Eric explained how they found the 'Angel Box' on their destroyed property, and how Julianna personally had seen it on the mantel here. Julianna bent down, rummaging through the contents from her purse. She grabbed the sweater, but the box wasn't there. All that remained was the pouch, her wallet, hair brush, keys, and makeup bag.

Anya watched her intensely. "Well? Where is it?"

"I don't know!" Julianna looked bewildered.

"It's right there," Lauren said, pointing to the mantel. The box was where it had been sitting before under the painting on the mantel. "I...I don't understand... we--"

Anya interjected, "Don't worry about it. It's just a prop anyway."

Julianna walked over to the fireplace and stared at the box. Sirens and people running broke the trance Julianna was in, and she turned around to see policemen running through the doors. Anya explained to the officers it was a misunderstanding. It took a lot of convincing, but, eventually, they left.

Anya turned to Eric. "Why didn't you just call me?"

"We didn't think you'd believe us."

Anya looked at him sternly. "Come here." She quickly lead him to a locked room. "In here." She tapped on the door. "This is where we keep all our props. Inside this door are dozens of paintings, furnishings, and about twelve angel boxes. Because, my darling, my movie is titled *The Angel Box*."

Eric, clearly shocked, laughed nervously.

Julianna and Lauren were speechless.

"What's that?" Anya asked, as she focused her attention on the pouch in Julianna's hand.

"It was with the Angel Box," she answered, handing it to Anya.

As Lauren was explaining that she was an accredited gemologist and the stones on the comb were real, Anya opened the pouch, and the comb fell out in her hand. It was beautiful and glistened with splendor while Anya gasped and turned it over in her hands. "Where did you find this again?"

Julianna started to explain again, but Anya cut her short. "My father gave this to me long ago. It was for my birthday. I was just eight."

She sat on the mahogany chair, her finger tips gently touching the precious stones. A single tear ran down her cheek.

"Where did you find it again?"

"It was at our brownstone that was destroyed by the tornado, under the rubble. At least the Angel Box was, but the pouch suddenly appeared in my purse after I'd placed the Angel box inside of it."

Julianna shuddered, and Anya looked at Julianna as if seeing her for the first time. Her face softened, and she seemed... different. The others didn't notice, but Julianna did. In that brief moment, a memory started to surface in her, but then was quickly gone.

"Oh, I see. Thank you so much for returning it. It means a lot." She grasped it to her chest. "It was always my favorite piece of jewelry, but then I lost it..." Her voice trailed off, and she had a far away look in her eyes as if she was back reliving that moment in time. She shook her head as if bringing herself back to the present.

They left the mansion and drove away for miles in silence.

Julianna finally cleared her throat and stoically said, "The Angel Box wasn't the same one. It was different."

There was nothing else to say. They dropped Lauren off at her apartment, then went home, not saying another word.

Chapter 12

THAT night, Eric tossed and turned in his sleep, but Julianna slept deeply, so deeply that it didn't seem like she was sleeping. She felt the wind blowing in her hair and the soft grass beneath her bare feet. She ran and ran through a field of brightly blooming wild flowers. Honeysuckle, lilies and lilacs were everywhere. She could smell their sweet aroma. She looked up to the bright blue sky as white billowy clouds covered the sun, and, for a brief moment, shaded the lovely meadow. She heard a little girl laughing close behind her and turned to see her sister running after her, her blond hair blowing in the breeze. She grabbed Julianna's hand.

"Come, Mum and Dad are going to give me my presents now. And we get crumpets and tea. Hurry!"

She pulled Julianna laughingly behind her. They ran up a hill to a grove of fir trees and plopped down on a soft green and beige wool blanket. Out from behind a tree walked a beautiful, tall, elegant young woman. Her blonde hair was piled high atop her head in a twisted bun. Her delicate features and high cheek bones made her look regal. She was carrying a white cake with pink candles flickering in the breeze. Her long white dress with a crimson sash made her look like a princess. Behind her was a tall, handsome man with dark, perfectly-coiffed hair with a bit of gray on his side burns. He had strong, sharp features and was wearing a gray suit and carrying brightly wrapped gifts in tissue paper.

Her sister jumped up and down with glee. "Oh, Daddy, may I please open just one before our cake?" she pleaded.

Her father laughed. "Alright. Just one."

He handed a small box to her. They sang "Happy Birthday" to her as she ripped open the tissue paper to find a pouch which she untied. A beautiful comb fell out onto her hands.

"I love it! I love it!" she squealed, as her mother quickly placed it in her golden locks. The man and woman kept singing, "Happy birthday, dear Emily..."

Julianna awoke with a start; she sat up and rubbed the sleep from her eyes. She could hear Eric puttering around in the kitchen. She smelled the freshly brewing coffee, and for the first time, she remembered everything about her dream.

Sitting at the kitchen counter in their small apartment, Julianna conveyed her dream to Eric. "It was so real," she went on. "You know, I've read about things like this: re-incarnation, people who have never taken a foreign language and under hypnosis or in their sleep, they can speak it fluently."

"Did you speak a different language?" he teased.

"Well, no!" she said, glaring at him, still shaken from her dream.

"Well, I don't know. Maybe you should go to a hypnotist."

"Really?"

"Well yeah. You know, I think there's one downtown by my office, Lady...something. Hopefully she not a quack."

With that, he started quacking and waddling around the kitchen like a duck. Julianna threw an oven mitt at him. She was totally annoyed, feeling like he wasn't taking her seriously.

"Well maybe I will," she said, pouring coffee into her

favorite cup that said, "Bad to the Bone," complete with a picture of a cute puppy. The toast popped up, and she yawned and grabbed the butter out of the refrigerator, slathered it on her toast, then added some chunky peanut butter, and took a huge bite.

"Want some?" she asked, covering her mouth, which was chock full.

"No, thanks," Eric yawned. He looked at all the moving boxes. "We've got to start moving this stuff to storage."

"No, remember, the Ericksons said we could put them in their barn."

"Oh, yeah, that's great, but it still means we have to do some manual labor," he groaned.

"Oh, suck it up, Eric," she sighed.

He walked out to the SUV with a couple of boxes, complaining the entire way.

Julianna quickly brushed her teeth and put on sweats, a tee shirt, and flip flops to help him finish loading. They started off to the Ericksons with both cars so full of boxes they could barely see out. Julianna called Charlotte to let her know they were on their way.

Charlotte was excited. "I have something to show you. Charles and I were talking--Oh, just get here as quickly as possible." Charlotte giggled.

As soon as Julianna hung up, her cell rang. She looked at the number, but didn't recognize it. "Hello?"

"Hi, Julianna," a man's voice answered, but it was breaking up.

"Hello," she said again.

"It's Dad. I'm in Peru, and I'm coming back to the states next week. I'd love to see you."

"Of course, Dad. I can't wait!"

"I'll call you from the airport when I get in on Wednesday."

"Ok, but, Dad, we're moving and…" She'd lost him.

When they got to the Ericksons, she told Eric about Charlotte's excitement and about her dad's phone call. Finally the dream evaporated from her mind. "This is a great day," she beamed.

Charles and Charlotte were on the veranda drinking lemonade.

"Come on up," Charles yelled down.

The housekeeper let them in, and they walked up the ornate stairway to the second floor.

"Hello," they said in unison and gave both Ericksons big hugs.

"We have a proposal. Please sit," Charles said.

The veranda's white decks shone in the summer sunshine. They sat down on a beautiful patio set. It was a wrought iron olive green with a glass tempered top. Huge baskets of beautiful flowers hung from every rafter, and the view was exquisite: the lake, the meadow, and the wild flowers. Startled, Julianna was reminded of her dream.

"Isn't it pretty?' Charlotte whispered.

"Yes, it's breathtaking," Julianna replied.

"About two hundred years ago, that was all forest, and you could barely see the lake. My Great-Grandfather and Great-Great-Grandfather logged it and built that barn and the out buildings. They added on to this old house--maids and servants quarters--and now we have a view," Charles reminisced.

As Julianna continued to gaze out at the meadow and the flowers, the memories of her dream flooded back.

"Eric, I'm going to the hypnotist," she whispered, and she walked over to the railing, pointing. "That's where it happened."

"What happened," Charlotte asked.

"Oh, Julianna had another dream last night."

"What about?" Charlotte also got up and walked over to the railing.

"It was right there in the meadow. It was a birthday party. I was Victoria, and it was my sister Emily's Birthday. My mother and father were there, at least they seemed like my parents. Anyway, they gave Emily a jeweled comb for her hair, the same one that was in the picture I found at the library. The weirdest thing is we found the comb. It's real, and it turns out it belongs to Anya Thorsen."

"The actress?" Charlotte was surprised.

"Yeah, the one I sold the Newlington Estate to." Eric stated."Remember all the weird things I told you before?" Julianna asked.

Charlotte nodded her head.

"Well, Anya's movie is called *The Angel Box*."

"No," Charlotte gasped.

Charlotte grabbed Julianna's hand. "Come, I need to show you something I just found. A diary was in a hidden compartment in an old chest we have in the attic. It's been there about two hundred years."

They walked up the three flights of stairs, past the third floor bedroom, and up to the attic.

"I was just reading it when you called me."

As they walked up to the attic, they saw everything was in disarray.

"Oh my," Charlotte exclaimed. "The window's broken again. We just had it repaired."

"There's blood," Julianna gasped.

Blood droplets were everywhere, leading to the top of the old chest where there was a small pool of blood.

"That's exactly where I left it!" Charlotte searched around the floor, pushing back old stacks of dusty books. "It's not here." She looked at Julianna. "I don't understand."

She sat down on an old rocking chair, defeated.

"Something came through the window and took it," Julianna concluded.

She went to the window, but she only saw how high they were, at least five stories up. The roof pitch would make it very dangerous for anyone to climb up there.

They both retreated down to the veranda, where Charles and Eric were discussing the economy.

"What's wrong?" Eric asked when he saw their perplexed faces.

"It's not there," Charlotte replied. "Someone stole it."

"What?" Charles was outraged as he walked towards them. "That's it; I'm getting a security system installed. Now that we've decided to stay, we need to make a lot of improvements."

"You're staying?" Julianna hugged them both, overcome with joy.

"Yes," Charlotte's eyes twinkled. "And remember how I told you we had something to show you?"

Charles interjected, "It's really a proposition." He winked and walked over to the railing. "Well, we feel like you're our kin. I know that seems strange since we haven't known you very long. It's just some people you…you just have a connection." He cleared his throat.

"What he's trying to say," Charlotte continued, "is we rarely see our own children, and they rarely get a chance to visit. We decided--"

"Only if you want to," Charles added. "You see there." He pointed to land overlooking the meadow and the lake to the right of where they were standing. "That's a five acre parcel we would be willing to sell to you at a fraction of the price. You could build your dream home, and in the meantime…"

"Live here with us." Charlotte piped in. Her eyes were dancing in anticipation.

"Really?" Eric asked, shocked. "You would do that?"

They both nodded with big grins on their faces.

"That's so nice," Julianna said, tentatively looking at Eric, her mind racing.

One part of her wanted to move there, and another part was afraid. If not for the dream she'd just had it would have been a no brainer, but she'd had the dream, and, frankly, this felt creepy.

"Okay, then," Eric exclaimed. "We need to talk finances."

Charles and Eric walked downstairs to the den. Charlotte grabbed Julianna's hand. "Do you think he'll go for it?" she asked.

"Well…if it sounds as good as Charles said…"

"Whoo-Hoo!" Eric's voice echoed from the den.

"I guess that's a yes," Julianna smiled, trying to seem genuinely happy.

Chapter 13

THE next week went by quickly as they moved their belongings to the Ericksons'. They decided to stay in the guest house adjacent from the main house. Mr. Erickson kept his promise of a new security system which encompassed the main house, barn, and entire surrounding estate. Between moving and doing her research, Julianna was exhausted.

Just as she was sitting down on the veranda on a chaise lounge to relax, her cell vibrated on the glass side table. She looked at the number and saw it was Lauren.

"What's up?" she answered.

"Well I miss you. Do you need any help?"

"Ha, great timing. I just finished," Julianna laughed.

"Do you want to grab a quick bite?" Lauren asked.

"Love to! How 'bout the sushi bar by the park."

"Okay, but let's eat inside," Lauren suggested, the bird attack still fresh in her mind.

"Of course," Julianna said consolingly.

As Julianna and Lauren were devouring California rolls, Julianna's phone vibrated again. This time she did recognize the number.

"Hello?"

"Hello, Julianna."

"Dad," she squealed as everyone in the restaurant turned

to stare. "Hi," she whispered sheepishly, slinking down in her chair. "I'm here at the airport. Can you come get me? I'm at the carousel waiting for my luggage."

"We'll be right there. What airline? Okay, see ya."

Her eyes danced, and they both ate the remaining sushi in record time.

"Lauren, can you come with me?"

"Right now?" Lauren was tentative.

"Well yeah. What's going on?"

"Well, I sorta made an appointment for you."

"With who?" Julianna eyed her as Lauren looked down at the table, embarrassed. "What did you do?"

Lauren turned red. "I took it upon myself to arrange a meeting with a psychic today at 2:00."

Julianna groaned.

"You'd bloody well better go. I'm out $200."

"You already paid for it?"

"Yes, I did, and you're welcome," Lauren smiled.

Julianna rolled her eyes then looked at her watch. "It's 12:05 now. I think we can just make it.

They both jumped into Julianna's VW and headed for the airport. As they drove up to the arrival gate, her dad was leaning against the wall, muttering to himself in deep thought. He was distinguished-looking, even though he was dressed like a home-less version of Indiana Jones, with a beat up old brown suit case with silver electric tape wrapped around it numerous times. His tall, tan, muscular frame was draped with khaki hiking shorts, a brown tee shirt, hiking boots, and a black fedora hat, with a large black backpack draped across his back.

"My God," Lauren exclaimed. "He looks just like Indiana Jones. Bloody hell." Julianna honked the horn making her father, who was still deep in thought, jump. Julianna threw her car in park, jumped out of the VW, and ran to embrace her dad.

"J-bird, I missed you so much."

She gazed up into his steel gray eyes and kind face. "Ditto," she said.

Then they did their traditional hand shake which consisted of hip bumps and an air spin ending with a chest bump.

Lauren watched from the car, amused, then grabbed her chest at the grand finale and murmured, "Ouch."

There were quite a number of people loitering around waiting for rides, plus constant honking cars full of irritated drivers. Julianna's dad hurriedly put the backpack and suit-case in the trunk. Her dad climbed in the back seat, his knees crammed near his chest. Lauren was in awe. Julianna was used to it. Whenever in the past her dad had been around her girl friends, they became mesmerized by his rugged good looks and boyish charm. He, on the other hand, never seemed to notice. Except for her mom, he'd never loved another woman, and now he was married to his work.

Julianna looked at Lauren's glazed over eyes and laughed. "Dad this is my best friend and colleague, Lauren."

She awoke from her enamored state and shook hands.

"Oh, aren't you the girl that was attacked by crows?" he inquired.

"One and the blooming same." She pointed to a bandage on her head and arms.

"Very strange…very strange indeed," he said, rubbing his scruffy beard. "You know, something similar happened about two hundred years ago, right here in Salem. But it wasn't just crows. It was animals, too. For some reason, it's as if they went mad, caused a lot of damage. People were killed. Very strange."

His piercing eyes stared at her, making Lauren turn around and shudder.

"Quit scaring Lauren, Dad."

"So sorry, Lauren. Please forgive me," he apologized. "We'll discuss it later on, okay?"

"Sure." Lauren smiled.

"Dad, Lauren has made an appointment for me to see a psychic. Do you want to come with us?"

" A psychic? Why?" Professor Hilard's brow furrowed.

"Some strange things have been happening, and this woman can take people back to different incarnations."

"Really?" His eyebrows raised in amusement. "I'm not going to say a thing," he chuckled teasingly as Julianna gave him an eye roll in the rear view mirror. "How about Eric? Maybe I can hang out with him."

"Okay, I'll give him a call. I know he'd love to see you and hang out," she laughed.

Chapter 14

ERIC was waiting for the girls and Professor Hilard when they arrived. The two men bear hugged, and Eric grabbed his father in-law's suitcase from the VW.

"You do know where they're off to, don't you?"

Eric gave him a blank stare

"A psychic."

Eric looked at Lauren and Julianna. "Really," he pondered. "Call me if you need me." Eric looked at his father in-law's puzzled face. "I'll fill him in on the details."

"Thanks, sweetie," Julianna said and gave them both a kiss.

Lauren and Julianna didn't have to go far. The psychic's office was just a couple blocks down from Eric's office. When they got there, the windows were covered with bright psychedelic graphics with the logo of a big eye and the words "Lady Lavonne's Spiritual Healing" in gold surrounding it. As they walked inside, a strong smell of incense seeped into their nostrils. The walls were covered with pictures from tarot cards and photographs of a woman with a scarf over her head standing by different celebrities.

"Wonder if these have been photo shopped," Lauren pondered as she stared at them.

"I wonder if she's a quack. Lauren, what have you gotten me into!" Julianna whispered.

Just then someone behind them cleared her throat. They both jerked around to see a woman.

"I assure you I am not a quack, as you so delicately put it, my dear."

Julianna turned beat red and began stammering how sorry she was.

"Don't worry, my dear. I get that a lot." She smiled, showing the many variations of gold and silver caps on her teeth. "But everyone is always satisfied after the session is over," she assured them.

She noticed Lauren's bandages. "Bird attack," Lauren blurted out.

Lady Lavonne knowingly nodded her head. She was tall, a regal bohemian in her seventies, slender with long salt and pepper hair that hung down past her waist. She wore a long gauze dress that had multicolored floral designs on it. Her feet were bare with a number of toe rings, brightly painted toe nails—every one a different color—and to top off this amazing homage to couture, a wreath of fresh flowers crowned her head. But what Julianna noticed the most was a silver pentacle necklace she wore around her neck. It was a serpent intertwined with blue stones in its eyes and a larger one in the center.

"You must be Julianna," the woman said, grabbing her hand.

As she gazed at Julianna's palm, Lady Lavonne suddenly jolted backwards and started chanting, lighting incense, and waving her arms in the air with the smoking sticks. Julianna and Lauren just stood shocked. Their mouths hung open, then Lady Lavonne suddenly stopped.

"I have never seen anything like this before. You have been touched by both good and terrible evil. The two elements are battling for your--" she whispered, "soul!"

Julianna gasped and grabbed her chest, finding it hard to breathe. It was as if something inside her was pushing on her lungs, collapsing them.

"Julianna," Lauren screamed before Julianna fainted into her arms.

When Julianna awoke, she had the thick stench of smelling salts under her nose.

"What happened?"

"You fainted," Lady Lavonne replied.

Lauren was standing over her. Black mascara smudged her face from crying.

"You had an anxiety attack. You'll be all right," Lady Lavonne assured her.

Lady Lavonne helped her into the back room where there was a round table with four chairs around it.

"Where's the crystal ball?" asked Lauren as she held Julianna's arm.

"Oh, I don't have one of those," Lady Lavonne chuckled. "Some people do though. To each their own." Then she looked at Julianna. "Do you still want to do this?"

"Well yes...I guess so. What did you mean when you said that?" Julianna whispered.

"Something, some great powers are around you, nothing like I've ever seen before. You can't control this...but maybe I can help you control the outcome." Julianna's puzzled look bore through Lady Lavonne's heart. "I'll try to help you figure this out."

She gestured for Julianna to lay down on her meditation couch. Julianna's fingertips traced the gold thread patterns in the purple upholstery. She glanced up at Lauren who had a fake smile that kept twitching.

"Lauren, you may sit down over there." Lady Lavonne pointed to a chair that was near the door. "So, Julianna, have you ever been hypnotized before?"

"No...never," Julianna whispered, swallowing the lump in her throat. "I don't know if I want to know I've lived before."

It's hard enough dealing with the present, she thought.

"Do you mind if I videotape the session?"

"No, not at all. How else will I know what happened?" Julianna nervously blurted out.

Lady Lavonne pressed the remote control for the camera above the door, and Julianna saw the little red light and heard the 'whoosh' sound of the camera as it tried to focus in on them.

Lady Lavonne's voice was low and monotone as she lulled Julianna into a deep sleep. Suddenly Julianna jolted and sat up. "It didn't work did it?"

"Oh, quite the contrary. You were out for--" she said, looking at the clock, "about twenty minutes."

Julianna sat silently, then looked over at Lauren. Lauren's eyes were as big as saucers.

"You bloody won't believe it, Jules," she whispered.

Then Julianna focused on Lady Lavonne.

"Julianna, would you like to see what happened?"

"Yes...absolutely. Lauren come sit by me." She was shaking as she grabbed Lauren's hand.

On the video she saw herself fall into a deep trance. Lady Lavonne took her back to a previous life and then asked her to describe where she was.

"I'm at my sister's birthday party," Julianna giggled.

Her voice and demeanor were that of a very young child.

"Describe your surroundings."

"We're in the meadow. It's so pretty and warm today. Daddy said it would be nice, but not hot enough to swim in the lake yet," she said, pouting. "We get to have a picnic, though, with fried chicken and shrimp salad, biscuits with butter and molasses, corn on the cob and birthday cake. Mommy made chocolate with butter cream frosting. It's Emily's favorite—mine too!"

"How old are you?"

"I'm ten, and my sister is eight today."

"What is your name?"

"My...name?"

Julianna watched herself look childishly at Lady Lavonne, then up at the camera.

"Well, my name, silly, is Victoria, Victoria Erickson."

Julianna's heart raced. *How could this be?* She felt her pulse pounding in her throat, which was dry and scratchy. Then her head began to throb, and she lay back down on the couch, curling up in the fetal position. She looked back up at the monitor and saw Lady Lavonne questioning her again. The little girl's soul was inside of her; she didn't even look like herself. Lauren sat by her, grasping her hand.

"Let's move forward a couple of hours," Lady Lavonne said. "Victoria, did you have fun at the birthday party?"

She saw herself start sobbing.

"No, we can't find Emily. She went in the water...We can't find her," she wailed.

"What happened?" Lady Lavonne asked, trying to console her.

"We were playing in the meadow," she sobbed, "and we

heard a funny sound...like chirping. Then we got closer, and it sounded like a lady singing. We looked into the lake, and underneath the water was a beautiful lady. She had long black hair floating all around her, and she smiled at us. She wanted us to come play with her, but we were afraid. We can't breathe under the water like that. Then she reached up out of the water and grabbed Emily. The comb that mommy and daddy gave her for her birthday fell in. Emily tried to get away, and I tried to help her, but the water got really swirly and rough, and she pulled Emily in, and then...they were gone. I screamed and ran to Mommy and Daddy."

Then Julianna collapsed, crying. Lady Lavonne told Victoria not to worry and counted to ten backwards, and then Julianna woke up. The video ended there.

Julianna sat up slowly, looked at Lady Lavonne and Lauren, and whispered, "Then it is real. I'm not imagining this."

"It is real and very dangerous. There have been many instances of people seeing something strange in that lake, and every time someone gets hurt or worse. There is great evil there. Many stories have been told about witches being flogged there. Evil spirits have been haunting it ever since. The last incident was back in the 1990's. A family of five—a man and his wife and their three adorable children. I knew them; it was a tragedy. The strange thing is that people on shore heard the odd sounds, then a woman's voice singing, a haunting eerie song. The water became very choppy, and the boat capsized. The woman was thrashing in the water, screaming at someone to get away from her babies, and her husband was fighting something. Then they all went under. They could never find the bodies. The rational explanation is underground current and caverns where they think the bodies may have been washed away, but they really just don't know."

"This is Erickson Lake you're talking about, right?" Julianna shuddered.

"Yes!" nodded Lady Lavonne.

"Oh God, we just agreed to buy the land next to it."

"You can't. You mustn't. Try to get out of it," Lady Lavonne urged, grabbing her shawl tightly around her chest.

"I don't know if we can. Eric was going to sign the papers today. I have to stop him." Julianna jumped up and hugged Lady Lavonne.

Lauren and Julianna quickly drove to Eric's office. They spotted Eric and Charles drinking coffee outside of the coffee house. Julianna and Lauren ran down the sidewalk.

"Where's the fire?" Eric teased.

"You haven't signed the papers yet, have you?" Julianna panted, out of breathe.

"Of course. That's why we came down here. We're celebrating!"

Eric held up a chocolate covered cookie and took a bite, but then he saw the look of terror in her eyes.

"Honey what's wrong?"

He stood up and embraced her. She burst into tears and started rambling about a boat, people drowning, and evil spirits in the lake.

"Wait, wait, wait," Eric said. "Slow down. What on earth are you talking about?"

He turned and looked at Charles who was as bewildered as he was. Julianna and Lauren began to explain their meeting with Lady Lavonne: the hypnosis, the past life, the boat accident, and the evil that lurks beneath the lake.

Charles was deep in thought. "Lady Lavonne," he muttered and shook his head. "She's the biggest con artist around."

Julianna stopped sobbing and stared at him. "What?" she murmured. "She's a con artist?"

"Yes, she leads you to believe crazy things by hypnotizing people, tricking their subconscious into saying and acting crazy, believing ridiculous stories."

"No, you don't blooming understand. I saw it. I was there," Lauren stammered. "She video taped it. It was real."

"Listen," Charles said sternly. "Lady Lavonne has been scamming people for twenty-five years. She's got a rap sheet twenty pages long: money laundering, forgery, petty theft, etc."

"No, you don't understand," Julianna shrieked.

The other customers turned and stared.

Eric shushed her. "Julianna get a grip. What the hell is wrong with you?"

Julianna couldn't contain her emotions any longer. She ran across the street with Lauren close behind her. Sobbing, Julianna and Lauren walked to the park where they heard a familiar voice behind them. It was her father. She turned, and he saw her face.

"What's wrong?" He ran towards them, and she collapsed in his arms.

"He doesn't believe me," Julianna wailed.

He helped her to the bench.

"Eric and Charles," she sobbed. "Charles said she's a quack."

"Who? The psychic?"

"But Dad, it was real. It really happened. She took me back."

She looked up at her father, her big brown eyes swollen

with tears. He wrapped his arms around her protectively, like when she was a little girl. Lauren continued to fill in the gaps of what had happened.

"Well, there's a very easy solution," he said, and they both grew quiet. "Go down to the police station tomorrow and find out if what Charles said is true."

"Why would she still be allowed to have her business here if what he said is true?" Lauren asked.

"Maybe it happened in a different state. I don't know," Professor Hilard speculated.

Charles and Eric walked up behind them.

"Look, Julianna, I believe you...about what happened, but as far as the lake being evil or haunted, I don't buy that," Eric said softly, stroking her hair.

Julianna sighed and looked up at him. She was worn out, but she felt safe again. She knew these people loved her, and she really didn't know anything about Lady Lavonne. Still, something seemed so familiar about her. She couldn't shake the feeling.

It was getting late and everyone was tired. Tomorrow, they would go to the police station and investigate Ms. Lady Lavonne to find out the truth once and for all.

Chapter 15

IT was 10:00 in the morning, a beautiful Friday. The air smelled clean and fresh from the cloud burst last night, which gave just enough rain to coax the final blooms on the cherry trees to open. The sky was a bright blue with some pretty strong wind gusts. Lauren and Julianna sat in the VW in front of the police station wondering if what they were about to do was necessary.

"Blimey, Julianna, we need to do this. We have to find out if what Charles said is true."

"But Lauren, you know I've been having these visions long before I even met her."

"I know, I know," Lauren answered.

Just then, four police cars and an ambulance sped past them. The sirens grew faint in the distance as they climbed out of the VW and started up the precinct's steps. As they walked through the glass doors, they could see quite a commotion. There were policemen running everywhere. Julianna's cell vibrated. She checked the number and saw it was Eric. Before she could answer, a very distraught African-American police woman asked if she could help them.

"Yes," they both said.

"Um..." Julianna continued, "we would like to speak--"

A young policeman ran up to the front desk. "Margaret, we

just got an APB about another homicide downtown. We need all the men we can get." Then he ran out the door, jumped in his car and with its sirens blaring, sped out of the parking lot. The police woman got on the radio and broadcast the information to any cars in the vicinity. She turned back to the girls, her brow wet with perspiration that she wiped with a Kleenex.

"Sorry, it's crazy around here. How may I help you?"

"We need to speak to someone about a woman who has a business here in town," Julianna replied.

"We need to know if she's legitimate," Lauren added. "We've heard she's a con artist."

"Let me see if I can find someone to help you."

She beckoned to a sergeant sitting at a desk through the adjacent window. He nodded his head, and she lead them through his door.

"This is Sergeant Thomas. He can see you now."

He was gangly, tall, and slender. He reminded Julianna of the actor Jimmy Stewart from her favorite Christmas movie, *It's a Wonderful Life*. He had a pleasant demeanor. He asked them to have a seat and offered them a piece of coffee cake.

"No, thanks," they politely replied.

They sat on the worn out wood chairs in front of his desk which was covered with pictures of what looked like his family—a pretty woman with blond hair holding two adorable toddlers, a boy and a girl. He noticed them looking at the picture and beamed.

"They're two and a half years old, Carly and Trevor, and my wife Janice."

"They're adorable," Julianna and Lauren cooed.

"We were wondering if you could help us? We were told

to check out a certain woman that we've done business with recently," Lauren said.

"And who might that be?" the sergeant asked.

"Lady Lavonne," Julianna replied.

"Yes, I know her well," he chuckled.

"A lot of people say negative things about her…but she has a gift. Before my wife and I ever got married, she told us about the twins—a boy and a girl."

He picked up the picture and gazed at it. "There have been many allegations made against her, but she's never been found guilty on any counts."

Margaret knocked on the window and pointed to her watch. There was a long line forming at her desk. The people in the waiting room were acting bizarre.

"I hope I've helped you ladies." He got up and walked to the door. "I'm sorry, but I need to help Sergeant Dewitt. Looks like quite a crowd is gathering out there."

He walked them out to the lobby where there were about thirty people crowded in the small area.

Hysterical and frightened, the crowd huddled together, searching for answers.

"Whats going on?" Lauren asked.

One of the men who was trying to console his wife said, "Some kind of animal—coyotes or dogs—went wild last night, breaking into houses and killing people."

Lauren and Julianna looked at each other, and again Julianna's phone vibrated. It was a text from Eric: "Urgent… call me."

When they got in the VW, she called him. "What's wrong?"

"Thank God you're okay."

"Why wouldn't I be? I'm at the police station inquiring about Lady Lavonne."

She put Eric on speaker. "You haven't heard?"

"No, what?"

"She's dead."

They both gasped.

"What the hell, Eric?" Julianna's face went gray.

"It happened last night. Some kind of animal or dogs broke through their windows downtown and attacked people, ripped their throats out."

Just then Sergeant Thomas knocked on the window, and they both jumped. Lauren clutched her heart.

"Eric, the sergeant is here. He needs to talk to us. I'll call you right back."

She rolled down her window. "We just heard. Oh my God!" Julianna gasped as she got out of the car.

"I need to know the last time you saw her," he inquired.

"Yesterday," Lauren said, walking up to them.

"About 2:00, then we left at about 3:15," Julianna added.

"I don't know what to make of this, but no one is safe till we kill those animals. It looks like a pack of wild dogs, about ten or more. You ladies go right home. Where do you live?"

"We're staying at the Ericksons' Estate."

"Nice folks," he said.

"I'm staying in my apartment north of here," Lauren explained.

"Just stay away from the downtown area."

"My husband's office is there."

"It's taped off. No one will be able to get in," he replied. "Be safe."

He turned and walked back in the chaotic precinct just as a white limousine pulled up.

"Ladies." They whirled around and saw Anya Thorsen sitting in the back seat, her window rolled down. "Did you hear the dreadful news about the killings?"

"Yes," they both said as they walked towards her.

Anya's hair lay in soft golden ringlets around her angelic face. "It's terribly frightening. It's going to scare my crew terribly. I hope it doesn't hamper production. We're due to film the debutante ball. In fact, we start filming in a couple of days."

Julianna and Lauren looked at each other in disbelief.

"I've got a fantastic idea. You must come and watch." The turquoise and fuchsia scarf wrapped around Anya's neck started fluttering out the cars window as a strong gust blew by. "Well ladies, do be safe. Ta ta!"

The limousine sped off.

"Can you believe that? The debutante ball?" Julianna whispered.

"It just gets bloody weirder and weirder," Lauren replied as she jumped in the VW.

"Lauren, I really wish you'd come to the Ericksons' and stay there with us till all this craziness is over. We could do research together about the Angel Box and the lake."

"I'd love to," Lauren responded, "but don't you think the Ericksons will mind?"

"Not at all. They'll love you…Please?" pleaded Julianna.

"Well, okay, but can I go and get some clothes and my laptop?"

"Sure," Julianna said, a big grin spreading across her face.

Julianna felt a calmness. Just knowing Lauren and all the people she cared about would be around her made her secure.

Eric couldn't go down to his office, but his work kept him so busy, she hardly ever saw him. Lately he seemed more and more distracted and detached. He was always with Charles.

Chapter 16

THE summer day was beautiful, so it seemed. The wind had died down and the summer flowers were in full bloom. As they left Lauren's and started for the Ericksons, the sky grew dark. Julianna looked up at the sky and saw a black cloud covering the sun. Lauren noticed it at the same time.

"That's an odd-looking cloud," she murmured.

The cloud soon was moving towards the Ericksons'. Julianna squinted at it as she drove.

"Lauren, I don't think that's a cloud."

"It's not," Lauren gasped. "It's bloody crows."

There were hundreds of birds.

"Oh my God, Lauren," Julianna yelled. "What's happening?"

The birds suddenly turned and were coming straight at their car.

"Go," Lauren screamed.

Julianna floored her VW toward the Erickson estate. The crows were getting closer, and soon they were swooping down on the car, smashing into it, denting the hood. The women were screaming as Julianna tried to keep the car on the road. Crows smashed into the windshield, blood splattering everywhere as Julianna turned on her wipers trying to see out, barely able to see the road. The birds kept hitting so hard they dented the doors and sides of the car. Then she crashed into the fence in front of the house. Lauren screamed as the jolt smashed her face into the dashboard. The birds kept pounding into the car over and over again, fracturing the windows. Julianna and Lauren crouched down in their seats, covering their heads. Julianna laid on the horn trying to scare them away, but the birds didn't stop. They seemed to be targeting only them.

The windows will shatter soon, Julianna thought, and she frantically began screaming for help. Then as soon as it started it was over. The windows were smeared with blood. Dead bird carcasses lay everywhere, some stuck on the windows, their beady black eyes open and staring at them. Julianna's car door was dented in so badly she had to kick it repeatedly to get it open. She squeezed out and went over to the passenger side as Charlotte and two gardeners ran to help her. The gardeners pried the passengers side door open and helped Lauren out. Her nose was bleeding. Dead birds were plastered to the car and covered the ground around it.

"Are you alright?" Charlotte gasped.

"Yes," Lauren stammered as she held the top of her nose with her head tilted back.

"Charlotte, this is Lauren. I've asked her to stay with us a couple days."

"Oh, I've I heard so many wonderful things about you," Charlotte said, rubbing her back.

Julianna's heart raced.

"I saw the whole thing. It was unnatural," Charlotte continued as they stepped over the dead birds, helping Lauren into the house.

"It's like they wanted to kill us," Julianna whispered. "Just like before."

There must be some kind of rational explanation, she thought, trying to remain calm. But the more she thought about the bizarre behavior of everything that had been happening around her, the more scared she became. She put her arm around Lauren as she helped her friend up the steps.

They went into the kitchen where Nellie was busily preparing some tea for them. Charlotte went into the bathroom and brought out a warm washrag and some cotton for Lauren's nose. Lauren wiped the blood off her face and hands and stuffed the cotton up her nose as she sat at the kitchen table with her head tipped back.

"Are you sure you're alright," Charlotte asked, as they all seated themselves at the table.

"I'm fine. Thank you," Lauren replied, smiling.

"I need to tell Eric what happened," Julianna said, swiping her finger over Eric's number. She felt exasperated as she left a voice mail about the accident.

"Charlotte, did you hear about the murders downtown?" Julianna asked

"Yes," she sadly said. "It's been all over the news. It's terrible."

Lauren and Julianna nodded their heads.

"Do you know who it was? They didn't say who the victims were yet because they needed to contact the next of kin."

Julianna looked at Lauren. "Well, I know one of the victims. We just talked to her yesterday." She hesitated. "It was the physic Lady Lavonne."

Charlotte gasped and put her hands to her face before bursting into tears. "Oh, no!"

Julianna and Lauren were stunned at her reaction since Charles seemed to dislike her so much; they thought she'd feel the same way.

"She was my friend. We've been friends since high school," she sobbed.

Julianna felt terrible and got up to put her arms around Charlotte.

"Charles didn't like her," she sobbed, "thought she was a trouble maker. Some things happened when we were younger. Lavonne instinctively knew and told me. I'm not going to go into details, but Charles and I broke up because of it, and he never forgave her." She paused and look sadly at them. "I secretly have been meeting with her every week since she moved back here five years ago. We were such good friends."

Tears streamed down her face as she dabbed them with a lace handkerchief.

"They say a pack of wild dogs did it," Nellie said as she put slices of carrot cake in front of them.

"What in the world is happening?" Charlotte sobbed.

"I know," said Julianna. "It's really weird. My dad said something similar happened about two hundred years ago."

"He's an archeologist," Lauren piped in.

Charlotte stopped crying and dabbed her eyes again. Both she and Nellie listened intently.

"He said the animals went crazy and killed a lot of people, and they never discovered why."

"Oh, my," Charlotte whispered, choking back tears. "You must bring him over here. I'd love to talk to him about it."

"Of course. He just flew in. He was on a dig in Peru."

"How fascinating," Charlotte replied. "How about dinner tonight? It will help to take my mind off of what's happened." She sadly stopped, changing the subject. "Nellie is making Cajun—her specialty. It's delicious." She spoke bravely, holding back tears.

She looked at Nellie, and Nellie smiled.

"Why did you go to Lady Lavonne's?" Charlotte inquired sadly.

"Because this one here," Julianna pointed to Lauren, "thought it would be a good idea and made an appointment. Anyway," she said with great trepidation, "I regressed back to a different time. I was Victoria Erickson."

Charlotte looked speculative.

"Then, she told us the lake was haunted and there have been a lot of drownings there."

Charlotte glanced at Nellie. Just then there was a rap on the door that caused them all to jump. Nellie answered; it was Carlos the gardener. He took off his hat, perspiration dripping down his face.

"Ms. Charlotte?"

"Yes, Carlos?" Charlotte got up and walked towards the door. "What's wrong?"

Carlos wrung his hat in his hands, looking terrified. "They're gone"

"Who's gone?" Charlotte asked.

"The birds." He looked perplexed. "The birds. I went to the barn to get the wheelbarrow and shovel, and when I came back... They're gone."

Nellie glanced at Lauren and Julianna as they walked to the door and made the sign of the cross across her chest as she muttered the Lord's prayer.

"Look, see." Carlos pointed to the car; the blood stains were there, but no crows anywhere.

"What's going on?" Julianna murmured.

"Carlos, just clean the blood up," Charlotte replied.

Julianna's phone vibrated. It was Eric. "Are you okay?"

"Yeah," she sighed.

"Okay, call the insurance company. Charles and I will be there shortly after we pick up your Dad. They've closed off the downtown area."

"See you soon. Be careful." Julianna felt more confused than ever but was relieved Eric, Charles, and her Dad would be there soon. It made her feel safer.

"Maybe the birds were still alive," Lauren speculated.

To take their minds off of the scary situation, they began leafing through magazines looking at different styles of houses and blueprints. The women consumed the carrot cake and chocolate chip cookies.

"You are the best cook, Nellie," Julianna said, munching on her third cookie.

"I think I've gained five pounds already," Lauren laughed, patting her stomach.

"Charlotte, you didn't get to tell me what you know about the drownings," Julianna inquired.

"Oh, that... Yes, there have been quite a few." She squirmed in her chair. "You see, the land across the way is a park owned by the state and it butts up against our land. The lake has dangerous undercurrents. In some places it's so deep that they haven't found the bottom. Scientists think it's an old dormant volcano."

"Well, Lady Lavonne told us that about twenty years ago a family of five drowned under very strange circumstances. The boat capsized in that lake."

Julianna all of a sudden felt very foolish.

"What's wrong Julianna?" Charlotte asked.

Charlotte looked very sad as she grabbed Julianna's hand.

"Uh...well, Lady Lavonne said it's...it's haunted."

"Oh, that," Charlotte sighed. "That's another reason Charles didn't like her. We've been trying to sell that land forever, and nobody would consider buying because of what happened."

Julianna and Lauren looked at each other. Nellie placed another plate of cookies on the table, and Lauren grabbed one.

"Is it true?" Lauren asked. "Is it haunted?"

Charlotte dabbed her eyes. "You know I don't believe that. It was just a terrible accident."

Nellie came over. "Would anyone like some more tea?" she asked holding the tea pot. They all nodded their heads, so she began to pour tea into the delicate floral cups.

"Lady Lavonne was a wonderfully gifted woman, but some of the things that she believed in simply were elaborated." Then she paused, trying to organize her thoughts and say what she needed to say as kindly as possible. "You see, she was a heavy drinker for years, until recently. She drank because she couldn't stand the pain. Her premonitions were so strong. She could see into the future, and it scared her. That's the reason she drank, to dull the pain. I know that's not an excuse, but it's the only way she could cope."

Lauren and Julianna finally had a new understanding. They realized why Charles reacted the way that he did, and Julianna felt badly for the way she'd acted towards him, especially since he and Charlotte had both been so kind to her and Eric.

Chapter 17

ANYA Thorsen was agitated as she spoke in her harsh demeanor to her lighting crew. "You must get it right," she dryly snapped, glaring at them. "We're running way over budget."

The crew was terrified of her. They needed these jobs and saw how she treated others, firing them when they didn't comply with her every whim.

"Anya, calm down," Doctor Swenson whispered as he walked up to her.

She glared at him. "How can I possibly calm down?" she whispered back. "You promised me you would find it, and you haven't kept your promise!"

"You must be patient Anya. It will work this time...It has to."

"You're right. It has to," she retorted back, "or you'll regret the day you were born."

He was used to her threats. He had heard them for far too long. He watched as she walked off in a huff. As he stood there immersed in the chaos, his mind wandered back to another time, another place. He remembered how it was before, before his life unraveled. He was once a country doctor, and he loved it. He interacted closely with people—going to their houses, meeting their families. His life then was very unlike the stark, sterile environment he had to endure now in his laboratory—working on experiments, horrible experiments for Anya.

He remembered how it first happened, his first encounter. It was a bright, sunny day. He had stopped at a quaint creamery shop. He was craving an ice cream cone. He remembered the tinkle of the bell on the door as he entered the shop. The black and white tiled floor shone with a fresh coat of wax as the sun bounced, reflecting off of it. The glass counters held every kind of penny candy one could possibly desire as well as the enormous wooden ice box where the clerk scooped ice cream out of the huge cartons onto his cone. His mouth watered just thinking of the old fashioned vanilla ice cream...It didn't taste the same now as it did back then. He could hear even now the churning of the ice cream makers, and he saw the clerk's wife pouring fresh black berries into it. It was August, and the blackberries were just ripe for the picking.

He saw two small girls. They were looking at the candy, their noses pressed up to the glass, trying to decide how to spend their precious few coins. He heard a commotion, then felt a tug on his coat and turned around. He saw the little blond-haired girl, her tear-stained face looking up at him.

"Mister, could you please spare a nickel? I dropped mine, and it rolled under the counter, and I can't get it." She burst into tears.

He squatted down so he was eye to eye with her. He noticed the unusual color of her eyes. They were a vibrant emerald. Just then, the other little girl walked up.

"Emily, you know Mommy and Daddy said you're not suppose to talk to strangers." Then she looked at him. "Sorry, Mister." And she curtseyed.

"That's quite alright," he said.

110

"But, Victoria, my nickel," she sobbed. "I dropped it, and it rolled under there." She pointed under the counter.

Anya's caustic voice brought Dr. Swenson out of his trance. "You'd better find it," she whispered in his ear, "because I will not go through it again."

She grabbed his jacket and began to shake him violently. Her strength was unnatural.

"I will not go through it again!" she screamed and stormed off.

Chapter 18

THAT evening, Eric, Charles, and Julianna's dad joined the women at the Ericksons. They all sat around the dinner table. The large dining room's elaborate mahogany table and velvet upholstered chairs were beautiful. The matching china cabinet had exquisite heirloom china in it. Julianna sat staring up at the chandelier.

"Do you like it?" Charles asked.

"Yes, it's beautiful" Julianna replied.

"I got it for the Swarovski crystals," he winked.

"Wow," Lauren and Julianna replied. It was the most beautiful chandelier either of them had ever seen.

"It was for our fiftieth wedding anniversary," Charlotte added.

They marveled at Nellie's wonderful Cajun cooking. They all were so full they could barely move.

"I should have worn my Thanksgiving pants, the stretchy ones," Eric laughed.

Everyone was content and full except for Charlotte; she'd barely touched her food. She was still deeply saddened by Lady Lavonne's death. Charles tried to console her, but she just wanted to be left alone.

On the veranda later that night, the women sat in the overstuffed patio chairs looking up at the crescent moon and twinkling stars in the clear night sky.

Charlotte confided in them. "She doesn't have any living relatives left, and I'm her closest friend." She took a hankie out of her pants pocket and dabbed at her eyes.

As they sipped their iced tea, they could hear the men in the den watching the news. Suddenly, Eric ran out to the veranda.

"They just killed them." He shuddered.

"Killed who?" Julianna questioned.

Charles and her father were close behind him.

"The wolves...about eight of them. They were right down the road trying to break in at the farm house."

They ran to the railing and looked to the west where in the distance they saw red and blue flashing lights from the police cars.

"Thank God," Charlotte murmured as she dried her eyes.

That evening, Julianna tossed and turned throughout the night, her dreams fragmented. She saw a wooded glen and an old shack. In her dream, she walked up the dirt path to the shack and stepped onto the porch. Creaking loudly, the rotted out boards gave way under her feet. It frightened her, but she wasn't hurt, and she was determined to see what was inside. She looked through the window pane but couldn't see through the thick grime. She took her shirt sleeve and rubbed the pane. Inside she saw a crude table and chairs with a flickering candle sitting in the center. No one seemed to be there. Slowly she opened the door; it creaked loudly. A foul stench filled her nostrils, and she gagged. Her heart beat wildly in her chest, as she tried to control her breathing. Stay calm, she kept saying to herself as she carefully made her way through the room. She picked up the candle and looked around. The room was all but barren, except for a fireplace with crumbling bricks. To the left she saw a small door, and she hesitantly knocked on it.

"Hello," she heard herself say. "Is anyone there?" Her voice was not her own, and it barely squeaked out.

She turned the handle, and the door hinges groaned as she entered the small room. The stench was overwhelming. Someone was lying on the bed. She put her hand up to her mouth as not to vomit. She smelled death and was afraid to look, but something caught her eye. Something was moving on the bed. She walked over, holding the candle closer to try and see better in the dark room. The moonlight cast eerie shadows on the wall from the outside window. She gasped as she held the candle down closer to the bed and dozens of beady eyes stared back at her before quickly scurrying towards her. Rats brushed against her legs. She screamed and dropped the candle on the floor as she jumped in terror. The candle started the throw rug on fire. She stomped it out and picked up the candle, which was still lit. There was an old quilt draped over a corpse. The body was still bloody with most of its flesh eaten away. Only remnants of a night gown still remained. The corpse looked like a woman with long brown hair, tangled wet with blood. The corpse was holding a black book, a diary. Prying the book from her cold dead hands made Julianna's skin crawl. She looked at the diary's black leather cover, but as she was about to open it, it disappeared, and she wasn't in the shack anymore.

She was in a cemetery, kneeling at a grave with flowers in her hand. It was dawn, and the sun was filtering through the trees. It was a small cemetery with only about ten gravestones. The names looked like they'd been crudely chiseled in the stone eons ago. The gravestone she was kneeling in front of had the name "MARY HASTINGS, born 1776, died 1792" chiseled on it.

Who was this person? Why was she there? Julianna wondered.

She heard methodical chanting over and over. It was coming from the glen behind her. She followed the sound of hypnotic female voices. They were in unison as they chanted. She crawled and hid behind a tree and looked down into the glen. She saw women with robes on, ropes tied around their waists in a circle, holding hands around a blazing bonfire. Their chanting continued as they raised their arms to the heavens.

Yahweh, Yahweh, Yahweh high
make the evil ones take to the sky
make them ground dwellers, that
ravage the sewer
make them mangy four footed
looters.
Take the evil and bury it away
Deep in the abyss down by the bay
Never to burden innocents with pain.
Yahweh, Yahweh never again.

The bonfire suddenly went out, and in its place was a golden box.

"The Angel Box," she gasped.

Its jewels glittered as if energized with power. Then, she saw some women coming from the lake. They were dragging a body into the circle, collapsing over it in sobs. Again the women started chanting. The last thing she remembered was a large white stag standing over her.

She suddenly woke up to the loud static of the T.V., and she fumbled for the T.V. remote, turning it off.

"Eric, Eric, you won't believe the dream I just had."

His back was to her, so she gently grabbed his shoulder and rolled him towards her. Rats were covering his body, chewing on his flesh. She screamed and started swinging her fists to get them off of him.

"What are you doing?" Eric yelled as he grabbed her arms.

"What—What's going on…Oh, Eric, you're ok."

She started kissing him.

"What's wrong with you?" he said, between kisses.

"I had the weirdest dream."

"Well you hit hard, too." He rubbed his arm.

"I'm sorry, honey. I guess I was still dreaming." She kissed his arm. "It was awful. There were women chanting in the woods and a grave and the black book…the diary." Her voice trailed off as his eyes glazed over. "I have to go and talk to Charlotte."

Julianna jumped out of bed and ran to the bathroom to change. Eric looked at the clock and saw it was 7:00 am. He rubbed his arm again. It was Saturday, and he wasn't about to get up yet. He yawned and went back to sleep.

A little later that morning, Julianna and Lauren sat in the kitchen drinking coffee and eating fresh baked scones Nellie had just whipped up.

"It's a good thing I'm wearing my sweats today after the nosh last night, Nellie," Lauren laughed as she snapped the elastic band.

It was a beautiful morning. The sun shone through the etched windows making colorful prisms on the kitchen wall.

"Blimey, that's too bloody weird," Lauren commented after Julianna finished telling her about her dream.

"Do you suppose that it really exists, the shack I mean?" Julianna whispered.

"What are you two whispering about?" Charlotte inquired as she shuffled into the kitchen in her blue terry cloth robe and white slippers. Her hair was in curlers with a bright orange and green scarf wrapped around her head.

"Julianna had a moony dream last night and we were wondering if there's a shack anywhere near here?"

"Well, yes. Not many people know about it. It's deep in the forest on state land. It's really run down. I went there when Charles and I were newlyweds. I think they were planning to tear it down, but they couldn't finance the parks development there. The recession, you know, put a damper on just about everything."

"Do you suppose you could take us there?"

"Yes, I'd love to. Let me get dressed."

Charlotte glanced at the clock and noted that it was 8:00 as she went to get ready.

Chapter 19

CHARLOTTE drove her silver Lincoln Towncar to the park on the other side of the lake.

"Charlotte, have you ever heard of someone named Mary Hastings?" Julianna asked.

"No, I'm afraid I don't recall that name. Who is she?"

"She was in my dream, I mean, her gravestone was, and I was kneeling in front of it with flowers."

"That is strange."

"I know. I don't understand what it's suppose to mean," Julianna sighed.

They drove down a gravel road until it came to a dead end.

"Now we need to hike up that hill, and hopefully it's still there," Charlotte explained.

The path was overgrown with sticker bushes and stinging nettles. When they got to the top, they saw the dilapidated shack. The roof was partially collapsed. Most of the boards were rotted out on the porch. Yellow tape blocking the entrance and a large sign was nailed to the railing: NO TRESPASSING--DO NOT ENTER--CONDEMNED. But the shack was what she'd seen in her dream.

Lauren looked at Julianna. "Are you crackers? We can't go in there. It's dangerous."

"Well I am!" Julianna ducked under the tape. She pushed

on the door knob, and it crashed inside, creating a billow of dust. The birds took flight as the crash echoed through the woods. Determined, Julianna entered the rickety building.

"Julianna, do be careful," Charlotte warned.

Inside, she looked around. It was just as she'd seen it in her dream. "Come on, it's not that bad."

Hesitantly, the women made their way into the dusty shack. Julianna went to the room where she'd seen the corpse. The door was propped open, hanging by a hinge. In the room was a crude bed with part of the roof collapsed onto it.

"It's not safe here," Charlotte whispered as a strong gust of wind stirred up more dust. The building swayed and creaked.

Lauren began sneezing. "Bugger. Dust and I don't get along."

The shack creaked again, and some more of the roof fell in on the bed. The wind was starting to blow harder.

"It's not safe. You're right. We need to go now," Julianna gasped.

Quickly they started for the entrance but Charlotte tripped and fell.

"Are you okay?" they both asked, helping her up.

"Yes," Charlotte said, brushing herself off. "Look, there's something," she pointed. "What is that?"

They saw a piece of parchment sticking out from under the floorboard. The board was loose. Julianna pried it up with her fingers. The parchment was no bigger than a couple inches, but what was underneath was what intrigued them. Stones were stacked on top of something. Painstakingly, they both lifted out the stones. Soon they saw it. Charlotte gasped. "It's the diary from the attic. I don't understand. Why is it here?" She looked at both of them.

"It was in my dream...It's real." Julianna lifted it carefully and placed it on her lap.

The wind began blowing harder.

"Come on. We'll look at it in the car," she said.

As they climbed back down the trail, a police car was parked at the bottom. A short, paunchy, balding deputy got out. "Howdy Mrs. Erickson, what-cha doing over here?"

"Oh, hi, Jerry. I was just showing my guests the spooky parts of Salem...the old shack."

"You'd better be careful. It's dangerous around here, what with the wolves and all," he replied.

"I thought they were killed!" Julianna replied.

"Well we thought so too, but the bodies, well, they just plum disappeared."

"Disappeared? What on earth?" Charlotte exclaimed.

"I know, it's weird. We turned our backs for a split second, and when we looked back, they were gone. The blood splatters were there, but the bodies weren't. They just plum vanished."

Just like the crows, Julianna thought. When she glanced at Lauren and Charlotte, she could tell they were thinking the same thing.

Chapter 20

A S they drove away, Julianna carefully pulled the little black diary out of her pocket and opened it up. The paper was so delicate and faded, the writing barely legible. In small handwriting, a name was inscribed: Annabelle Hastings.

The first entry was
The Year of our Lord April 1784,

My sister and I shall go with mother today to gather herbs and berries in the glen. Mother used them to make medicines and elixirs to help the sick. Maybe if we're lucky we'll find some mushrooms...we're so hungry. After father disappeared food has been scarce.

Mother has been trading remedies for food; she has always had a healing touch. People from all around bring their sick children to her for God's nectar as she calls it. I don't know what it is, but it seems to help the poor sick babies.

She turned the page.

When we were picking berries yesterday Mary found something in the bushes. It was a box, but it won't open, and as she carried it, it started to shine. She brought it to mother. Mother looked scared and wouldn't touch it. Mary's hands were shiny like the sun. The box was so pretty with little children with wings and shiny stones. Mother said they were angels. Mary's hand tickled and kept shining. Mother told her to put it down, so Mary did, but the shiny went all over her body. Mother was so scared and told us never to speak of it and hid Mary in her room until the shiny went away.

Next page.

Mother fell sick today and her breathing is labored. Mary is tending to her. Mother is feeling much better now. She says Mary is a miracle, she has healing hands. Many others have died from diphtheria.

A little girl went missing today. People say the evil in the lake got her. Some say it was the Devil's Daughter. It scares me... I've heard her sing. So has Mary. Some think that a witch was flogged and that her spirit is taking revenge. The little girl was found barely alive. She has pneumonia.

The little girl's father heard about Mary and took her to the big house to help his daughter. Mary took the herbs and tonic that mother suggested. Emily Erickson seems to be much better now.

Many pages in the Diary had been torn out and were missing.

Mother said we must be careful. People are talking. They are envious of the admiration towards Mary. They call it evil and ungodly, the devils work. Mary can cure people and it scares them.

Mr. Erickson came to our home today and brought a wrought iron bed with a goose down quilt. Mother was so happy, she cried... She never cries. We slept very well last night.

More pages were ripped out.

There is talk of witches...We hear many strange noises at night. It scares us. We sleep with Mother.

The year of our Lord 1792

Many children have gone missing; everyone is afraid. Mother and other Wiccans from the neighboring areas were in the glen tonight, holding hands around a bonfire. The Angel Box appeared as they chanted a prayer. People are saying that Mary is a witch and she is possessed by the Devil. They are saying it about many who heal the sick.

They have taken many poor souls to town, charging them with heresy, doing the devils work. Everyone is afraid. Mother is afraid they'll come for Mary; she just sits praying in her room.

They took Mary yesterday and have found her guilty. They are going to flog her till she admits to being a witch. I must help her; I must find the box and show them that it is God's work.

I went to the glen and looked in the bushes. I found the box. Maybe now they'll believe me. I picked it up with my shawl, so the shiny wouldn't get in me.

It was too late for Mary. My heart is cold. Mother and I touched the box.

"That was the last entry," Julianna said.

The car was silent.

"They flogged a young girl, those monsters," Charlotte sobbed.

"In my research," Lauren stated, "the Salem witch trials

only lasted six bloody months, six months before the judge realized that what he was doing was sacrilegious. But what I don't understand is that was in 1692, not 1792!"

Julianna shook her head. "I don't understand either, and I didn't realize that the Angel Box was found here. I thought it was found on a dig somewhere exotic like Peru...not here!"

"We really need to ask your father about this," Lauren said.

Julianna looked back down at the dairy. It had disintegrated and was just dust in her lap.

"It's gone," she gasped. "Our proof."

They drove back to the Ericksons in complete silence.

Professor Hilard rubbed his chin as Julianna, Lauren, and Charlotte explained the diary to him.

"So, where was the Angel Box first discovered?" Lauren asked.

"No one really knows. It's been mysteriously showing up all over the world. But I do believe it was somewhere here in North America," Professor Hilard speculated.

"I'll google it." Lauren grabbed her phone, her fingers flying over the keyboard. "Here it is." She started reading, "It says here that the first documented evidence was in North America...Salem, Massachusetts."

"You were right," Julianna smiled and hugged her Dad.

"It was in the 1600's," Lauren continued. "Then the Smithsonian Institute in Washington DC acquired it in 1906 from the Ericksons. Two months ago they started touring with it and other antiques. When they got here, it went missing. There was an investigation, and the police could find no evidence of a break in. It says here that this often happens; it just goes missing." Lauren looked at them and shrugged.

Professor Hilard continued. "We've studied it. It's an

enigma not of this earth and has energy comparable to radiation, but it's not radiation. Scientists have been baffled for years about these results. The box doesn't open, but radiates a golden aura. Now you know why it's my favorite artifact. It's an anomaly!" Professor Hilard exclaimed.

Chapter 21

CHARLOTTE decided to stay home because she was very tired. Lately she had no energy. *Too much excitement,* she thought as she lay down on her comfy bed.

Eric had gone to work after they had opened up the downtown area. Julianna texted him about her plans, but he didn't reply. Lauren and Julianna borrowed Charlotte's car and drove to the mansion. They were still in awe of its grandeur and amazed at the amount of cars, trucks, and people milling around. The pasture to the east of the mansion was littered with movie vans and large trailers.

As they wandered into the large foyer, they were starstruck by all the beautiful costumes and famous actors and actresses. They went though the library to the Grand Ballroom. The actors had on turn-of-the-century ball gowns and suits. Anya spotted them and glided over in her baby blue satin gown, her hair in an up-do with the jeweled comb they had given her securely in place. It startled Julianna, and her mind was jolted back to what she'd seen in her vision. She felt uneasy as Anya grasped her hand. Anya kissed both their cheeks and thanked them for coming as they both nervously giggled.

"I'm so glad you made it," Anya gushed.

"What gorgeous gowns," Julianna responded.

"Yes, we have an excellent costume designer: Roberto

Cantese. He's designed for all the great films and even won an Oscar for the movie *La Bottega*."

Julianna and Lauren were impressed.

"I see you're wearing the comb," Lauren noticed.

"Yes, thank you for returning it to me," she said as she fixed her hair.

"It looks lovely," Julianna added.

Anya smiled.

Julianna was still reeling from the entire scene. It was exactly a recreation of the vision she'd experienced and the picture she'd seen at the library—the dress, the comb…Emily Erickson.

Just then Doctor Swenson walked in, looking agitated. He took Anya aside and talked in low whispers. She started raising her voice, then he reminded her where they were. Lauren and Julianna heard him say, "It will be alright…we'll have it soon." Anya calmed down and let out a sigh of relief.

The director screamed in a high pitched voice, "Places, People. Places. You extras spread out and you--" He pointed to Julianna and Lauren.

Anya interrupted, "They're with me. I invited them, Josh."

He looked exasperated. His tall, thin frame was draped stylishly in a gray suit. He wore Louis Vuitton loafers and a purple fedora tipped to one side, hiding his slightly balding spot.

"Well, that's just fine," he said coolly, "but they need to get out of the shot."

Lauren and Julianna went to the far side of the ballroom and watched as the beautiful dance sequence unfolded. The choreography was breathtaking as the men and women waltzed in and out of perfectly synchronized formations. The dancers seemed to glide gracefully as if on ice, rising and falling with each melodic crescendo of the orchestra. When it finished, the director yelled, "Cut! That was perfection, people. Good work." Everyone seemed pleased with themselves and went to change for the next scene.

"I wonder what the doctor and Anya were talking about?" Julianna whispered to Lauren.

Chapter 22

DR. Swenson left Anya and went out to the rose garden. He was tired. The years were going by slowly, and he saw no end in sight. Why him...

It's because of her, he bitterly thought. *I couldn't harm a child, even knowing what I know now.* He sat on a bench by the rose garden and put his head in his hands and wept, remembering the day that changed his life forever.

He was twenty seven years old, having lunch at the local diner. He heard a commotion outside; people were running and screaming. His waitress ran out the front door to see what was happening. She came back in and frantically announced that a little girl, Emily Erickson was missing and presumed drowned in the nearby lake. Doc threw money on the table, grabbed his medical bag, and rushed out the door. He and many other townsfolk ran down to the lake. Emily's parents, the sheriff, and others were in the lake wading up to their waists frantically searching for her. Little Victoria was on the shore hysterically crying. A neighbor lady picked her up, trying to console her. Some of the men had gotten boats and were paddling out to the middle of the lake. Emily had been missing more then an hour.

Then he remembered one of the boat's oars hit something, and the man started yelling. One of the men dove into the lake, and soon surfaced with Emily's lifeless body. The other men then hoisted her onto the boat. They quickly brought her ashore where Doc started compressing her chest. He turned her onto her stomach and continued pushing on her back trying to express the water. He was astonished when she started coughing and sputtering. When he turned her over, she started kicking and swinging her arms wildly, trying to get away. Her pupils were dilated, making her eyes completely black. Emily's parents stood over him, watching as the doctor brought Emily back to life.

Victoria broke away from the lady who was trying to console her, and pushed her way through the crowd to her sister's side.

A horse drawn buggy transported Emily, Doc, and her family to their home. Emily was on the verge of death; she had pneumonia and a high fever. For days she was in and out of consciousness as Doc stayed by her side.

Mr. Erickson heard of a young Wiccan who had an extraordinary gift of healing. He went to the small shack in the woods and begged for help. He promised to take care of Mary Hastings and her family, pay her handsomely if she would agree to try and save Emily's life. Mary was brought to the Erickson's home, and in front of Doc and her family gave Emily an elixir and laid hands on her. What they witnessed was the most amazing moment of their lives. When Mary put her hands on Emily's chest, they began to glow, and the radiance went into Emily. Her chest and lungs lit up with a brilliance, and the light healed her.

Mr. and Mrs. Erickson fell to their knees and sobbed as Emily's breathing improved. Her fever was gone, and she made a full recovery. Mr. and Mrs. Erickson were so grateful to Mary, they paid her with four guinea.

As Doc and Mary rode his horse back to her home, he inquired, "How did you do that Mary?"

"I don't know!" she answered shyly, whispering, "It's not me. It's them."

"Who?" Doc asked.

"The angels—they do it through me."

Doc was confused, so he decided to ask her mother. Mary's mother was also very vague. It was if they were hiding something. Bewildered, Doc left the shack and was riding home through the glen. At a distance he saw Mary's sister, Annabelle. She was placing something in the bushes. At first he thought she was picking berries, but then she quickly ran back up the hill to her home. He went to the spot she'd been kneeling at. He saw nothing at first, then the sun came out from behind a cloud and streamed in through the trees. Something shone brightly under the brush He pushed the sticker bushes away. He saw it… It was a small box.

In hindsight he wished he'd never found it, never touched it. All it had done was caused the evil to live, the evil in Emily. The lady in the lake was real…pure evil. Part of that evil was in Emily, and he and Mary had saved her. Now he needed to save himself. For he was Doc Briggs back then, and Anya was Emily, and what she was about to do was unimaginable.

"Mother, I hid it just like you told me," Annabelle said as she ran through the door.

Mary was sitting at the table eating rabbit and mushroom stew.

"Annabelle, look, look what Mr. Erickson gave me." She pointed to the guinea on the table. Annabelle's eyes grew wide with wonder; she'd never seen that much money before. Their mother came over, sat down, and grabbed both the girls' hands.

"We must give thanks to God," she said. "God has given a great gift to Mary, but we must be careful. God please protect our family and let Mary's special gift be used for good to help sick and helpless souls and never used for evil."

They had no idea what Mary had just done, what evil the world would soon see, the horrors that she had unleashed.

As Doc picked up the small box; the shiny went up his arms. He felt it enter his entire body, and he began to shake violently, convulsing as if having a seizure. He lay unconscious in the forest for more than an hour. He came to when rain began pelting down on him. His horse nuzzled him on his back, and he managed to get up on his hands and knees. He was dizzy and felt nauseated. The box sat beside him, but it was no longer glowing. He took his coat off, wrapped it inside, and managed to climb onto his steed. It started hailing; thunder and lightening lit up the sky. He barely was able to stay on his horse as it galloped wildly through the forest to his small cabin.

He tethered his frightened horse inside the barn and grabbed his coat with the box wrapped safely inside. He staggered into his one bedroom home as the wind whipped through the trees, sending branches flying constantly hitting the outside of his small cabin. He placed his coat with the box inside on the table then lit a candle and placed it near the box. He threw some more wood on the fire and collapsed into his favorite chair before falling into a deep sleep. When he awoke, the box was gone.

Five years passed, and the evil in Emily lay dormant. Doc watched as little Mary had her thirteenth birthday. Mr. Erickson kept his word and took care of Mary and her family. The old rotted out shack was transformed into a cozy two bedroom cottage with a new outhouse.

The Ericksons felt such gratitude that they asked Mary's mother, Elizabeth, to work for them as a housekeeper. Mrs. Erickson was with child and was very weak and bed ridden. It was a very difficult pregnancy, and Elizabeth Hastings was a great asset to the Erickson family. Mary and Annabelle spent many hours helping their mother at the Ericksons'. They became best friends with Emily and Victoria. They were all very close in age and spent countless hours playing in the woods by the glen and at the Hastings' cottage. But their favorite times were spent in the attic having tea parties and playing dress up with Mrs. Erickson's old clothes she stored in the wooden chest.

One day as they were playing in the glen, Annabelle went over to the berry bushes where she'd hid the box. Annabelle looked in the bushes, expecting to see the box, but it was gone. "Mary, it's not here."

Mary, Emily, and Victoria ran over to where she was kneeling.

"What's not there?" Emily asked.

"The Ang…" then Annabelle stopped, putting her hands to cover her mouth.

Mary looked frightened. Emily and Victoria looked at both of them, bewildered.

"What are you talking about? What's an Ang?" Victoria asked.

"Nothing," Annabelle answered, her face turning red.

"Mary what's an Ang? What's Annabelle talking about?" Emily asked.

Mary just shook her head, not saying a word. Emily squinted her eyes at Mary, trying to see what she was hiding.

"Mary, tell me what she's talking about." She pushed Mary down.

"Emily, quit it!" Victoria screamed.

By that time, Emily was sitting on Mary's chest, holding her arms down.

"Stop," Annabelle screamed.

"No, she's going to tell me!" Emily started slapping and hitting Mary.

Mary started crying as Emily continually slapped her and screamed at her. Victoria and Annabelle tried to pull Emily off of poor Mary. Emily had never acted like this; she was crazy. They couldn't budge her; she was incredibly strong.

Mary screamed, "Stop it," and her arms began to glow. She forcefully pushed Emily who flew through the air and landed with a thud ten feet away.

"Don't you ever do that again, Emily Erickson," she sobbed and curled up in a ball on the ground.

Emily was furious. She got up, dusted her clothes off, and ran back to her house.

From that time on, the sisters never played together again. In their adolescence, they became bitter enemies. Emily was controlling of Victoria, and if she even mentioned the idea of talking to Mary and Annabelle, Emily would go into a tirade. Her rage was so violent, it terrified Victoria. Through time Victoria let it go. Even though she longed for her friends, it wasn't worth the repercussions.

The Ericksons thought it was just a childish argument that would remedy itself, but that never happened. Emily kept her distance from Elizabeth, Mary, and Annabelle. The girls never visited the Ericksons' home again.

Mrs. Erickson gave birth to a beautiful baby boy which they named Charles after his father, and all their focus was mainly on him.

Years passed, and Emily and Victoria became beautiful young women. As Emily drew nearer to her sixteenth birthday, her parents prepared for a debutante ball. Two years prior to this, Victoria had celebrated her sixteenth birthday and in turn had met the love of her life, Stephen Anderson. At the elaborate ball they had caught each other's eye. Emily was jealous of her sister and had a secret crush on Stephen. He was tall and handsome with blonde hair and a muscular physic. Emily was a great actress in hiding her feelings, and Victoria had no idea.

Stephen was twenty years old, an honest, kind man. He was a carpenter making beautiful furniture. Victoria was so happy and felt like the luckiest girl in the world. Stephen proposed marriage after six months of courting, and Victoria couldn't wait until they would wed.

Chapter 23

EMILY was furious about the wedding but continued to hide her rage. She finally went to Elizabeth and stated her regrets. She pretended she was sorry for all of her transgressions towards Mary and all the bad blood it had brought between their two families and kept apologizing over and over again. Then she confided to Elizabeth that she'd fallen in love with a boy and how he didn't seem to notice her at all. She wondered if there was a perfume that she could use to get his attention. Elizabeth understood young love and thought it was sweet. She did have some lovely scents with lavender and rose water, so she told Emily to go to the cottage and ask Annabelle and Mary. So Elizabeth wrote a note for Emily to give to her girls so they would find just the right scent for Emily. She went to the cottage not only to get the perfume, but also under the pretense of make amends with both Mary and Annabelle. But Emily was seething inside; the evil was coming into its own, and she had to be careful to hide it.

She walked up the steep embankment, muttering to herself the entire way, trying to contain the wrath inside her. She gingerly knocked on the door. Mary answered it, taken aback by Emily's presence.

"Emily what...what are you doing here?" she stuttered.

"Mary, I thought it was time I apologized for my bad

behavior. It was childish and utterly demoralizing to both of you. I'm so sorry for my actions. Please can you find it in your heart to forgive me?" she said as a single tear trickled down her cheek.

Annabelle had come to the door and heard Emily's apology, but she didn't trust Emily and saw through her facade. Then Emily thrust the handwritten note from their mother into Mary's hand. Mary and Annabelle read it. Annabelle rolled her eyes and went back to her cleaning, realizing the only reason for Emily's behavior was because she wanted something. Mary, however, was so innocent and naive that she truly believed Emily's apology.

As Mary lead Emily to the small shack behind their cottage where her mother kept medicines, elixirs and plants, Emily spoke to her as if nothing had ever happened between them, confiding to her about the fictitious boy who she had a crush on that didn't notice her and how badly she wanted him to come to her debutante ball. In turn she also invited Mary and Annabelle, offering to lend them beautiful dresses to wear if they needed them. Mary kindly thanked her for the invitation.

As they walked into the small shack, Emily saw rows and rows of shelving with bottles for every aliment you could imagine. The lavender and rose water scents were in the back, high on the upper shelves. As Mary took the step stool to the back, Emily's eyes scanned the bottles. She found what she needed, a love potion. She quickly grabbed the small bottle and placed it in her coat pocket. Mary soon returned with the scent. "Here, I hope this helps." Emily handed her a small gold coin. "No, Emily, it's a gift…I'm so glad were friends again," Mary said, hugging her.

Lately the smell of people——no matter if they'd just

bathed—nauseated Emily, and she had to hold back her will to vomit.

"Thank you, Mary. That's so sweet of you," she lied. "Maybe we can talk some more tomorrow."

Mary smiled, and Emily went home. It was Sunday and the Ericksons always had a huge midday supper after church.

"Emily, where were you this morning?" her mother asked as Emily walked in the door. "Pastor gave a wonderful sermon today."

"Oh, I took a walk," Emily lied. "I wasn't feeling that well and thought the fresh air would do me good."

Victoria and Stephen entered the dining room and sat down at the table. They were having a large pork shoulder roast, and the smell permeated through the house. An abundance of turnips, potatoes and carrots surrounded the succulent roast along with Mrs. Erickson's famous homemade applesauce. As everyone sat down and joined hands around the beautiful mahogany table to give grace, Emily could hardly contain her hatred for the love between Victoria and Stephen. It made her sick; she couldn't even look at them. Emily reached down and felt the potion in her dress pocket.

"Mother, may I be excused?" she asked.

"Certainly, dear," Mrs. Erickson answered.

As Emily briskly walked towards the kitchen, her father's late arrival almost knocked her down.

"Emily, dear, I'm so sorry. I should have been here earlier. Are you alright?"

Emily was furious but controlled herself. "Daddy, it's not your fault. I should have watched where I was going."

As her father steadied her she felt a cold liquid running down her leg. *The bottle*, she thought quickly. She went into the kitchen. The cook was busy putting fresh green beans into a bowl. She reached into her pocket and drew out the bottle. The lid had come off, and there was just about half an ounce left. *Hopefully it will be enough*, she thought as she poured it into a glass of lemonade. As she entered the dining room with the tray of drinks, she placed the glass with the potion in it in front of Stephen and then gave the rest to her family.

"Emily, how thoughtful," Mrs. Erickson gushed.

"Cook is so busy, I thought I'd help her."

"Well, it was very sweet," her father replied as her mother tended to baby Charles.

Stephen and Victoria gingerly picked up their glasses and began to drink. Emily held her breathe. Stephen drank all of his in one gulp. Emily had to control her glee. Suddenly the effects of the elixir started to take hold; he slumped over the table.

"What's wrong, Stephen?" Victoria cried.

All Stephen could do was grab his stomach and groan. Mr. Erickson helped him into the parlor and laid him onto the divan, Victoria by his side holding his hand as he writhed in pain.

"Father, go get Doc," Victoria sobbed.

Mr. Erickson hurried out the front door and galloped away on their fastest steed.

All of a sudden, Stephen sat up. His moaning ceased, and he grew very quiet. He opened his eyes, sweat beads dripping down his forehead. His eyes were blurry, then he saw Emily standing over him smiling. It was the most beautiful smile he'd ever seen. Someone was holding his hand; it was Victoria. She looked worried and plain, not at all like she'd seemed before. He was confused at what was happening. Emily seemed like an angel, a beautiful angel. The more he gazed at her, the more beautiful she became. He reached for her, pushing Victoria aside. Victoria was shocked as her fiance pulled Emily down to his side and began kissing her passionately.

Mrs. Erickson came into the parlor, holding Charles in her arms. She gasped as she witnessed Emily and Stephen while poor Victoria ran out the door. "What are you doing?" Mrs. Erickson screamed.

Stephen couldn't talk; he was still in a haze. Emily looked at her mother with a sadistic smirk on her face.

"What, mother…can't you handle the truth? Stephen doesn't love Victoria. He never has. He felt sorry for her. He loves me now, and there's nothing you or anyone else can do about it." Then she laughed and began kissing him again.

Mr. Erickson and Doc entered as Mrs. Erickson ran upstairs crying, carrying baby Charles.

"What's wrong?" he asked, puzzled, as he and Doc witnessed their blatant behavior.

"The truth," Emily said simply, as she ran her fingers through his blonde locks.

"What truth?" Mr. Erickson's voice boomed.

"About Stephen and I," she smiled sarcastically. "Our love, it's finally out in the open. We aren't going to hide it anymore." She sighed.

"What are you talking about?" he yelled.

"We've been in love for a long time. We were afraid to tell… but now." She looked at Stephen who gazed adoringly back at her. "But now you all know the truth." She smirked.

Her father and Doc were in disbelief. Mr. Erickson ordered Stephen out of the house. Doc helped him to his horse. He was queasy and clearly not himself. Doc rode him back to his house and laid him on his bed. Stephen fell into a deep sleep.

Mr. Erickson searched for Victoria and found her sobbing in the loft of the barn. He tried to console her, but she was inconsolable.

Chapter 24

AT the movie set, Julianna and Lauren were awestruck by the enormity of the production. The beautiful sets were carefully thought out, down to every detail of the period. Special effects were done in front of a green screen. Actors magically seemed to grow twice their size, transforming in appearance to hideous creatures with fangs and claws. Julianna and Lauren got to see the amazing makeup artists work their magic behind the scenes, sculpting prosthetics to cover the actors' faces and bodies. Latex strips were adhered to the witches, making their skin a greyish green color with boils and blisters. Contacts were put into their eyes making them all black.

Even though they didn't want to admit it, Anya was a wonderful actress. In one scene she saved a woman from being flogged; in another she was testifying in a courtroom at the Salem witch trials.

The story was about her family being persecuted, accused of being witches. The evidence was their possession of the Angel Box which was thought to be evil and always seemed to appear at the killings.

The director asked for a closed set, so Julianna and Lauren exited to the rose garden. The fall sky was clear. A beautiful evening, the brisk air smelled clean from the shower that had just stopped hours before.

Stage hands were working feverishly behind the enormous hedge. Julianna and Lauren peered through the bushes, startled by what they saw. A piling was formed about five feet high, made from rocks and hay with a platform of wood with tall stakes rising up on top of it. Rope shackles dangled down, the breeze making the ropes thump against the wooden posts.

"That's just creepy," Lauren gasped.

"I know. I wonder which character gets to experience that," Julianna whispered.

"I don't know, but I'm not going to come back to see it," Lauren shuddered.

"Me either."

They both left the mansion and begin driving back to the Ericksons'. Lauren was fumbling with the radio as Julianna drove the windy road. The road was treacherous, a steep cliff to the left and woods to the right on a very narrow road. Julianna could barely see, it was so dark. There were no street lights and only her headlights lit the way.

Suddenly, Lauren turned down the radio. "Did you hear that?"

Julianna grasped the wheel tighter. "No...what?"

"Blimey, I heard something queer."

A loud snarling echoed through the darkness and seemed to be getting closer to their car. Julianna floored it and soon saw the lights from the Erickson's mansion. As they drove further from the woods, the growls grew fainter, then disappeared altogether, leaving Lauren and Julianna shaken to their cores. They drove into the garage and waited for the door to close tightly before they cautiously got out.

"I need a piss up," Lauren sighed.

"What?"

"I need a drink," Lauren explained.

"Ditto," Julianna agreed.

They entered the house. There was a quiet serenity as they walked toward the den. Everyone was gathered around the T.V., even Nellie who still had a potato and knife in her hand, captivated by what the reporter said.

"The recent attack by animals is not only happening on U.S. Soil, but everywhere in the world," the reporter announced. The television's broadcast showed London streets inundated by large rodents scampering everywhere. They had gotten into the food supply. The rodents were very aggressive, biting and spreading disease. It was the black plague all over again. The army was shown trying to combat the nasty varmints with flame throwers to no avail; they simply disappeared. Eric was clearly uncomfortable and grateful Julianna was there. Julianna and Lauren grabbed some wine coolers from behind the ornate bar in the den. Then they went to sit in front of the T.V. with the others on the large leather sectional. They sat and sipped the wine coolers nervously as they listened to Julianna's father reminisce about how he'd studied the animal killings two hundred years ago.

"It's very much like what happened before," he explained. "The animals went crazy everywhere, killing and maiming everything in sight."

"What happened? How did it stop?" Julianna asked.

Charles answered, "It stopped when they killed a witch, not an innocent by any means, but an honest-to-God Devil-worshiping witch." He paused.

"She was the epitome of evil. At least that's what the transcripts of the trial said," added Julianna's father.

"Charles, please don't do this," Charlotte pleaded.

Eric, Julianna, and Lauren just looked at each other.

"You've got to be kidding me," Julianna gasped. "I thought you were going to tell me something scientific, not this ridiculous garbage. This can't be the reason it stopped." "Oh, but it is," Mr. Erickson sheepishly stated. "You see my ancestors are the ones who killed her, at least his men did."

Lauren and Julianna were shocked. Charlotte cringed and left the room. Charles looked sadly down at the floor.

"Now you know the horrible secret that has been passed down all these centuries. Charlotte doesn't believe that the girl they killed was evil, but she was."

"It was a girl?" Julianna gasped in horror. "Wait, when did this happen?"

"The late 1700's, as I recall," her father answered.

"That's mental! It doesn't make any sense. The Salem Witch Trials were in 1692," Lauren added.

Julianna looked at both her father and Charles. "You mean, years later they were still killing people."

"You have to understand," Charles tried to explain. "Children, dozens of children were disappearing. Some they found, some they didn't. They were brutally murdered, Julianna. My ancestors did what needed to be done."

Julianna was inconsolable and ran into the empty kitchen where potatoes were boiling on the stove. She smelled roast chicken cooking in the oven. Charles and her father followed her, persuading her to go back to the den. Nellie passed them in the hallway, explaining how everything was going to go to "Hell in a handbag" if she didn't finish supper.

"Julianna, I know this is upsetting," Charles said.

She sat down by Eric, and he put his arm around her and

gently kissed her on the cheek. They all sat and listened as Charles told the history of his ancestors.

"The stories my Great-Grandfather told me were terrifying. He was a very old man, but his memory was surprisingly intact, especially about these events. They were very clear in his head. He was just a little boy, only about four or five years old. A number of his friends went missing. There were a group of women who lived in shacks in the forest and some in a cave. They formed a coven who worshiped the devil. My Great-Great-Grandfather was a wealthy man; he tried to help some of the poor lost souls before this happened. He was scared, as all of them were, and formed a collusion of men to try and search for the children. What they witnessed was terrifying— the women sacrificed the children in the name of Satan to gain strength and power. They found remains of the children in the cave, some mummified. That was enough evidence for them to proceed to capture and bring the women to justice. They had a trial, found them guilty, and put them to death."

He paused. "The leader was a young girl. She wouldn't die. They tried everything, and finally they succeeded."

Julianna and Lauren were appalled. "We don't want to hear anymore," Julianna whispered, looking at Charles.

"That's how the killings by the animals stopped," her father added.

Julianna put her hands over her mouth. "I feel sick." She ran to the bathroom.

Lauren squirmed in her seat. "We heard growling on the way here. It was in the woods."

Julianna came back into the den. "I'm going to go check on Charlotte. Charles, I know it's not your fault...it's just a lot to take in."

He nodded understandingly. Charles looked at Eric, Lauren, and Professor Hilard. "I think its time we secure the mansion."

He left the den and met with his staff to execute his plan. All the mansion's five stories of windows were secured by unlatching the shutters from the outside walls and securing them tightly over the windows. All the doors were dead bolted and Julianna, Eric, and the rest of their guests were to stay in the mansion until the threat was gone. Even the old hound dogs who usually slept outside on the porch in their fancy dog houses were brought in. Julianna watched as the dogs sleepily sauntered in and plopped down on rugs in the laundry room.

She looked at Eric and Lauren. "Yeah, those two will really protect us," she laughed.

As she talked to Charlotte in the kitchen, Nellie served them some hot tea. Charlotte sighed. "Well, now you know. That's what broke up Charles and I so many years ago. But he still justifies it. To this day he thinks it was the right thing to do. They killed a bunch of homeless women and a young girl!"

"But, Charlotte, what they found in the cave," Julianna whispered.

Charlotte put her hand up to silence her. "They were self appointed vigilantes, and they murdered those poor homeless women," she cried, "but he believes they did the right thing." She was clearly very distraught and went to her room.

Julianna was exhausted and also very sad to find out about the Ericksons' past. She was connected, and it scared her. After all she seemed to be the reincarnation of Victoria Erickson; she was kind of a relative too. That is what really was bothering her, but she dared not bring it up again. It would make her sound too crazy.

That night, Julianna had a fretful sleep. She dreamed of the women in the forest, the chanting, and the girl they dragged out of the lake. But her dream continued on. The girl was revived. She wasn't dead but was alive. It was Mary Hastings.

The next thing she knew, she was climbing up the hill in the Glen. She could barely see. It was pitch black. She came to an entrance of a cave. She could see a faint glow inside. She removed the brambles and branches camouflaging the entrance. She heard something and leaped behind some trees. She saw Mary, her mother, and sister go inside the cave. This must be where the witches had their coven. *Why would they go inside such a wicked place*, she wondered. Then her dream catapulted her deep into the cave's belly where she hid behind a large rock. She heard whispering and saw the glow of a fire with three figures huddled around it. She smelled potatoes and carrots cooking in a stew. A cast iron pot bubbled over the open fire. Mary was cutting up more carrots and potatoes. Annabelle and her mother were busy skinning and gutting a large rabbit they had trapped.

As she crept closer, the whispering became more audible. Mary asked her mother "When can we go back to the cottage?"

Her mother shook her head. "Never, I'm afraid. It's too dangerous," she said as she put the cut up rabbit into the stew. Then she wiped her hands on a tattered cloth. "Mary," she said softly. "Dear, they tried to kill you."

Mary looked at her solemnly as tears ran down her cheeks.

"That's why we had to put the gravestone up, so no one will ever hurt you again… They think you're dead."

Annabelle grabbed a brush and sat behind Mary, brushing her hair.

Her mother went on. "That's the reason we had to move

our belongings down here. They are convinced Annabelle and I have left."

Mary wiped the tears from her eyes. "Mother, why do they hate me so much?"

Her mother shook her head. "I don't understand either. I don't know what or why they think you had anything to do with any of it."

Annabelle stopped brushing Mary's hair and began to braid it.

"Mother," Annabelle whispered. "I think someone told the men that Mary did it, someone they trusted."

Mrs. Hastings shuddered. "Who would be so wicked to accuse an innocent girl, someone who has always done good, someone..."

She stopped and gasped. She knew, she finally understood as they all did. In that moment the truth was hard to believe, but it was the truth, and Emily was the culprit. Mary just sat there stunned.

"This place will protect us for now. No one dares to come down here. They're too afraid," Mrs. Hastings whispered.

Mary buried her head in her mother's shawl as she wept. Stroking her daughter's hair, she gently rocked back and forth, trying to console her. "The men buried the children's remains, and hopefully the witches are gone. All we can do is pray to God to show us the way to protect ourselves."

They sat in silence and stared at the fire's orange and yellow flames licking at the cast iron pot.

Julianna awoke and remembered everything.

Chapter 25

THE next morning at the kitchen table Lauren and Julianna sat, barely awake.

"I need coffee," Lauren moaned, and Julianna poured her a cup. "Thanks."

Nellie was puttering behind them and took fresh baked banana bread out of the oven; the aroma was heavenly. She drizzled a maple glaze on top of the cream cheese frosting, setting the pieces on the table.

"You'd better let them cool," Nellie warned as they both grabbed for them, burning their finger tips.

Julianna placed her fingers in a glass of water, then dried them off and sighed. "Lauren, we need to go to the woods, by the shack. There's a cave there."

"What?" Lauren smirked. "Yep, that's exactly what I bloody wanted to do this morning...Hey, maybe we could also go skydiving without parachutes. Sounds fun!"

"No, Lauren, I had a dream last night, and..."

"So you think because you had a dream, we should go scampering in the woods when there are killer rats, crows, and wolves waiting to murder us? Yeah, sounds smart and bloody fun!"

"But, Lauren..."

"No. Are you mental?"

"Shh," Nellie whispered, scolding them. "You two need to be quiet. You'll wake Ms. Charlotte."

Julianna glared at Lauren and watched as she nibbled her banana bread. Julianna drank her coffee and began eating her banana bread, afraid to mention the trip again. "I know it's dangerous," she whispered as she took another bite, "but I need to find the answers."

"What are you talking about?" Lauren angrily asked, and she scoffed, "Why people do bad things?"

"No, why these memories are coming back to me…why the animals are killing people."

Lauren stared at her, knowing Julianna would just go by herself.

"Okay. Bloody hell, Julianna, I wish you'd quit having these stupid dreams. It's crackers!" she said, as she grabbed another piece and stuffed a huge bite in her mouth.

After Lauren gave in, they begged Nellie not to tell anyone where they were going, especially Charlotte.

"Don't you worry. I'm not gonna give Ms. Charlotte another thing to fret about, but you two promise to be careful," she warned.

They both nodded to reassure her, even though personally being scared to death.

As they walked towards the barn, Julianna pondered, "The crows are only a threat in the day, so we should wear bike helmets, maybe take some rope." She paused.

"And a big bat to smack those suckers," Lauren suggested.

"That's my girl," Julianna smiled.

In the barn they gathered their equipment: flashlights, rope, a Swiss army knife, bottles of water, and some flares. They put everything in the back of the SUV, then proceeded back to the house.

The men were in the den drinking coffee in their bathrobes. Charles had his nose in the paper checking the stock market reports, Julianna's dad was on his laptop, and Eric was channel surfing between football games and world news.

"Honey, would it be okay to take the SUV to town for some errands?"

"Sure," he said, his eyes glued to the T.V., not even looking at them. He was definitely in the "Sport Zone." Julianna rolled her eyes.

They went to change into hiking clothes. Julianna made it out to the SUV first and warmed it up. She started channel surfing herself, trying to find an interesting talk radio show. Then she saw her. *What in the world*, she thought.

Lauren was walking towards her. She had on swim goggles, an old army coat, cowboy boots, a bike helmet, a large back pack, a rope draped over her shoulder, and a bat. As Lauren got in the car, she noticed Julianna's shocked expression.

"What? This is a dodgy deal. Better safe than sorry," she smugly stated.

"Ok," Julianna laughed. "You look ridiculous. What are you wearing? Really?"

She couldn't stop laughing; her laughter was contagious, and Lauren started laughing, too. Tears were streaming down their faces, and they couldn't catch their breath.

Soon they were driving towards the old shack. They drove over the covered bridge towards the state park.

"I can't believe it's October already," Lauren sighed.

They looked at the beautiful red and orange leaves on the trees. Some even looked florescent in the morning sun.

"This is my favorite season," Julianna added. "I just wish the leaves wouldn't fall off. They're so beautiful."

The park was full of joggers, many with their dogs.

"Blimey, it's like none of them are worried about what's happened," Lauren noticed.

"I know, it's weird... They'd be worried if they saw you," Julianna teased, and Lauren laughed.

Julianna turned down a dirt road to the right of them and tried to dodge the large pot holes. They soon came to the hill where the shack was, and Julianna parked behind some bushes. The "No Trespassing" signs were a constant reminder they shouldn't be going up there. They looked around, got their equipment out, and shut the door quietly. They proceeded to start the long, brambly climb up the trail. When they got to the top, they walked past the shack going north about a quarter of a mile.

"We have to be getting close," Julianna said, stopping to rest with her hands on her legs. "I'm really out of shape," she gasped.

"Well, I'm no better," Lauren said, chugging the bottled water. "I'm absolutely buggered."

"I know it's around here; I feel it" Julianna stated.

They both started poking around.

"I think that's it." Julianna pointed to a thicket to the left of where they were standing.

Lauren took her bat and cleared away the brambles. Then they lifted the pile of rotten logs away as a large centipede scurried out.

"Blimey," Lauren screamed.

"Shh," Julianna whispered.

There was the opening. They'd found it; now they had to

muster up the courage to go inside. They got their flashlights out and cautiously ventured inside the small opening. They had to duck down at first, but as they went further, they were able to stand up. They traveled down a long dark tunnel. It opened up to a small cavern. They shined their light around on crumbling remnants of long ago abandoned furnishings. They inspected every inch of the small cavern. In the cave, there was a tunnel that went even further in. They traveled down it but soon came to a dead end. As they walked back towards the center of the cave, Lauren saw something and picked it up.

"It's a drawing, a blooming bunch of drawings."

It was yellow, tattered parchment paper with women on them. The initials "A.H." were written at the bottom of each one. Julianna looked at Lauren and whispered, "Annabelle Hastings."

Julianna stopped. "Shhh...Lauren be quiet. What is that?"

She heard children's voices whispering a nursery rhyme she recognized. Julianna could barely make it out. "Do you hear that? The children—do you hear them?"

"No, Julianna, you're scaring me."

The nursery rhyme became more audible, the small voices chanting over and over again: "Ring around the Rosie, pocket full of posies, ashes, ashes we all fall down."

Julianna began to look around frantically. "Where are you? Can we help you?"

Then finally the voices were so loud, she covered her ears. All the while Lauren looked on helplessly. Then silence.

"They're gone," Julianna gasped. "You couldn't hear them?"

"No," Lauren shuddered. "Come on, let's hook it. This place gives me the creeps."

Julianna and Lauren ran back out into the sunlight.

As they drove back to the Ericksons, Lauren asked, "Do you want to tell me what that was all about?"

Julianna shook her head. "I...I heard voices, children's voices, and they were saying, no chanting a nursery rhyme."

She explained what she heard to Lauren.

"That's macabre. That's about death, Julianna. I think the posies were supposed to protect them, ashes were their cremation, all fall down, they died."

"Why would I hear something like that?" Julianna asked.

"I don't know, but that cave had bloody horrible things happen in it, and I never want to go back there again." Lauren looked at Julianna.

"Neither do I."

Lauren gazed down at the drawings. "You know, this seems odd, but wouldn't these have disintegrated like the diary?"

"I don't know. Maybe the paper is different," Julianna added.

She pulled into the Ericksons' driveway, and Lauren handed the drawings to her.

"You're right. These look new. How can that be?" she pondered. "They look exactly like I pictured them."

Eric tapped on the window, and they both jumped.

Julianna rolled down the window. "What are you trying to do? Send us into cardiac arrest?" she snapped.

"Sorry," he laughed. "Hey, where did you get those?" He snatched the drawings from Julianna's hands.

"Uh, we went on a hike."

"I thought you went on errands."

Eric's stare and raised eyebrows made Julianna feel guilty.

"Okay, we went to the cave, alright. We found them there."

"Why in the world did you lie to me, and why are you two poking around caves when nobody's safe?"

"That's why we didn't tell you, because I didn't want to listen to a lecture," Julianna angrily said, getting out of the SUV.

Eric backed up and raised his hands. "Okay, Okay, I surrender. I just worry about you."

He planted a passionate kiss on Julianna's mouth.

Lauren walked over to them. "Get a room," she said teasingly.

Eric laughed and looked at her. "What are you wearing? Nice duds," he teased.

"Better safe than sorry," she responded.

Then he looked at the drawings again. "So how do you know the Hastings? You know, I just found a rental house for them."

"You what?"

"I found them a house."

"What? Wait, these people? You found them a house?" Julianna's face turned white.

"Well, Julianna, they're probably relatives," Lauren explained.

"You're losing me," Eric sighed.

Mr. Erickson yelled out the door. "Eric, come on. We're going to be late for our tee time."

Eric looked at Julianna. "Go on you big goof," she teased before kissing him.

He sprinted off toward the house.

Julianna looked at Lauren and asked, "How is this possible? Three relatives that look exactly like them."

"How do you know that, Julianna?" Lauren sighed.

"My dream," Julianna murmured.

"Well, I say we go find them and show these drawings to them and see what they have to say."

Julianna nodded.

They went and changed their clothes into more suitable attire. Charlotte was taking a nap, and the men were leaving for golf. Nellie was in the kitchen kneading dough, and Carlos was outside with his crew manicuring the hedges.

They found the listing on Lauren's phone and set her navigation to 1209 NE 13th Raven Drive.

"Bloody creepy address," Lauren commented.

Julianna nodded her head.

"Hey, where are you guys going now?" Eric asked as they drove past.

"Girl stuff."

Eric raised his eyebrows. "You're going to see the Hastings, aren't you?"

Julianna laughed. "Yeah."

"Well, tell them hello. Please don't freak them out."

"Of course not," Julianna scoffed. "Why are you still here?"

"We were too late for our tee time, so we're going to practice putting," Eric explained. Mr. Erickson had a beautiful putting green that they were practicing on. The girls drove off as the men concentrated on their game.

Chapter 26

A S they drove to the address, Julianna couldn't get the children's voices out of her head. Why did she hear them? It must be a message.

"There it is!" Lauren exclaimed.

Julianna pulled up and parked in front of a little yellow house. It was neat and tidy with a small, manicured lawn. Geraniums sat in the red window boxes on either side of the black door. The front deck had a rocking chair made of branches wrapped with twine. Soft cushions brightly upholstered with a floral print sat on the chair. Three angel wind chimes hung down from the porches rafters; their musical tones filled the silence with each wind gust.

"This is so quaint," Julianna said as she and Lauren walked up the steps to the front door. She hesitantly knocked on the door and waited.

"I don't think anyone's home," Lauren whispered.

They looked through the front window, then suddenly heard a car drive up behind them. A woman and two girls got out of a beige mini van.

"Can I help you?" the lady asked while carrying bags of groceries.

"Mrs. Hastings?" Julianna asked.

"Yes." She looked startled.

"Um, my husband is Eric Hawthorn of Hawthorn Realty. He found this house for you, and we were just wondering how you were getting along."

"Oh, how kind." She looked at her two daughters. "We're just fine, thank you."

"Oh, good," Julianna said, nodding her head. "By the way, I'm Julianna and this is my good friend, Lauren."

She shook her hand, and Lauren waved awkwardly.

"Please, let us help you with your groceries," Lauren said, as Mrs. Hastings walked up the front steps trying to manage three bags.

She gladly let Lauren and Julianna hold the bags as she unlocked the front door. Julianna and Lauren couldn't believe how much the drawings of them were spot on. "Please, do come in," Mrs. Hastings graciously offered.

"Thank you," Lauren and Julianna responded as they walked into the tidy house.

The living room and kitchen were just one room with a dining table sitting to the left of the kitchen. Mrs. Hastings took the groceries from Julianna and Lauren and set them on the kitchen counter as her daughters did the same.

"The reason we're here besides seeing how you're getting along--" Julianna hesitated. "It's because we found something of yours."

"At least, Eric seemed to think it might be yours," Lauren added as she pulled the drawings carefully from her coat pocket.

Mrs. Hastings gasped as Lauren handed them to her. Her daughters peered over her shoulder and became frightened.

"Where did you find these?" the young girl asked.

The younger daughter's eyes were a vibrant blue which

seemed to pierce through them as she stared, waiting for an answer. Lauren was speechless.

"In the woods," Julianna stuttered, "by the old shack. They were in the bushes."

The older girl looked at them suspiciously. The silence was awkward as the Hastings just stared at them.

"Well my husband saw these and thought we knew you," Julianna explained.

"Why don't you ladies have a seat, and I'll get you some lemonade. Would that be all right?" Mrs. Hastings asked.

"Yes...sure," Julianna agreed, fidgeting with her keys. They sat down at the kitchen table.

"I drew them," the oldest girl exclaimed.

"Well, you're a wonderful artist," Julianna responded as Mrs. Hastings sat lemonade in front of them.

"I'm Ann, and this is my sister Mary."

"It's so nice to meet both of you," Julianna and Lauren exclaimed.

Mary just sat, staring at them. They drank their lemonade in awkward silence.

Then Mrs. Hastings got up from the table. "Well, thank you so much for visiting and bringing us the drawings."

"Our pleasure," they said, as Mrs. Hastings showed them out.

Julianna and Lauren waved goodbye as they drove off, leaving the Hastings staring at them from their front porch.

Mary Hastings looked at Annabelle and her mother. "They know," she bluntly stated, her face stone cold.

They both nodded.

"What do we do now?" Annabelle whispered.

"We talk to them," Mrs. Hastings responded. "We just talk

to them," she murmured again, trying to grasp the severity of what they needed to do.

"She's connected…the missing piece," Mary whispered as she twirled her hair between her fingers. Her eyes glowed with wisdom. Her mother and sister knelt at her feet.

***

"It's them," Julianna exclaimed as she grasped the wheel.

"Blimey. How can this be happening?" Lauren asked. "It's impossible. They'd be more than two hundred years old."

Julianna turned on the road back to the Ericksons'.

"I know. It's the box…It has to be. Everything is somehow connecting, and it's scaring me Lauren. I feel…"

"What?" Lauren whispered.

Julianna had never been so frightened in her life. "Something catastrophic is going to happen, and I don't just feel it, Lauren." She pulled up to the Ericksons' driveway, pressed the garage door opener, then pulled into the garage. She looked sternly at Lauren. "I know it, Lauren. I don't know how or why or when, but it'll be soon."

Lauren just stared at her. Then they hugged each other. Lauren knew she was right. "God help us," she whispered.

Chapter 27

JULIANNA and Lauren were still shaking as they walked into the Ericksons' house. Charlotte was in the kitchen talking to Nellie about what to prepare for dinner. She looked pale and was still in her robe. She smiled as they walked in.

"Charlotte, aren't you feeling well?" Julianna asked as she walked over to Charlotte.

Charlotte shook her head and made her way to the table, slowly sitting down on a chair. "I don't know what's wrong. I just feel so light-headed."

"Maybe we should take you to the doctor," Lauren suggested.

"No, no...I'll be fine!" Charlotte responded.

Nellie just shook her head as Charlotte got up and shuffled out of the room. Julianna followed close behind her.

"She's been like this on and off for more than a month now," Nellie sighed.

Nellie had a large turkey sitting on the counter. She began seasoning it.

"She refuses to go to the doctor or even tell Charles."

"Well, I'm going to tell him," Lauren responded.

"You can't," Nellie said, as she placed the turkey in the oven.

Lauren became indignant. "Why not?"

"They're not here. They're off playing golf."

"Oh, that's right. Of course they are," Lauren scoffed. "You know the bloody world could literally be ending and the men would go and play frigging golf!"

Nellie laughed. "Ain't that the truth."

Lauren went to find Julianna who was pacing outside of Charlotte's bedroom door.

"How's she doing?" Lauren asked.

They both heard a loud thud. Lauren and Julianna looked at each other. Julianna knocked frantically on the door. "Charlotte are you okay?" There was no answer.

She opened the door, and to their horror found Charlotte lying in a pool of blood. She had struck her head on the corner of the night stand when she fainted.

"Lauren, go get Nellie and call 911."

Julianna was frantic. She ran to the bathroom and got a wet washrag to try to stop the bleeding from the gash on the side of her head.

Charlotte regained consciousness. "What happened?" she whispered.

"You fainted and hit your head."

Charlotte looked solemnly at Julianna. "Tell Charles--" Then she grimaced in pain and grabbed her chest. "That I know...I've always known...Tell him..." Her voice trailed off.

"Tell him what?" Julianna said frantically.

"Tell him--"

Just then, Lauren and Nellie ran in the room. Julianna put her ear close to Charlotte's mouth as Charlotte whispered to her. Julianna's eyes grew wide and she began to tremble. Then she let out a wail. "No! You can't go! No!"

She frantically began CPR. The sirens in the background

grew louder, and Nellie went to let the paramedics in as Lauren fell to her knees sobbing.

It was too late; Charlotte was gone. The three women watched the paramedics work frantically over Charlotte, trying to revive her to no avail. Then, they watched in horror as they zipped the black bag over her body and wheeled her out on the gurney.

Charles ran in, still in his golf cleats, and stopped the paramedics in the hallway. They heard his sobs, then his anger. Their hearts were broken.

Wandering out into the hallway as if in a horrible nightmare, the three men were in shock. Charles sobbed uncontrollably as he continued to follow the paramedics to the ambulance. The rest of them sat stunned in the hallway, not saying a word.

Julianna broke the silence. "They said she had a heart attack."

"What did she say to you?" Lauren asked.

They all looked at Julianna.

"It didn't make sense. I really need to tell Charles. Maybe he'll understand."

She hugged Eric tightly, and they both began to cry.

Charles walked past them and up the stairs to the bedroom. He stood looking out of the window as Julianna came up behind him. He was staring out at the lake, not realizing she had come in. Julianna touched his shoulder, and he turned towards her, his face red and eyes swollen from crying.

"Oh, Julianna, they said it was cardiac arrest. I don't understand; she never had trouble before."

He sat down on the bed and buried his head in his hands.

"There's something I need to tell you. Charlotte made me promise, but it sounds irrational."

"What?" he asked, puzzled, his brow furrowed. "She told you something, before she..." and his voice trailed off. He became sad and withdrawn again.

"It doesn't make sense." Tears streamed down her face.

Charles looked solemnly at her, waiting to hear what his beloved had said.

"She said," Julianna swallowed the lump that had lodged in her throat, "that the devil's daughter will end it all unless you find them. Then, she said we must find the key."

"What?" he exclaimed and began to laugh a maniacal laugh. Then he grew very quiet.

"What did she mean?" Julianna asked tentatively.

He shook his head and got up and started pacing.

"It's a crazy old wives' tale that's been passed down through generations."

Much of what he was saying Julianna had already heard.

"The devil was cast out of heaven, and he stole one of God's most beloved possessions, The Angel Box. He descended to Earth, forming a crater which was Erickson Lake. The lake used to be called 'The Devils Daughter.' The tale went on to say that the Devil hit the earth and split in two, creating a female counterpart. He went to the nether world, and she stayed on Earth, for all eternity in the lake."

He cleared his throat. "That's how my Great-Great-Great-Grandfather acquired this land. He homesteaded it. Nobody else would touch it. He knew it was hog wash, just a crazy myth. Then bizarre, crazy things started happening."

"But you said..." Julianna interrupted.

"I know what I said." Charles cleared his throat again and looked sadly out the window at the lake then back at her. "The accidents could be rationally explained. Nothing happened for years, then--" He paused, sat on the bed, and looked down at the floor, his tears trickling down. "The accident...the boat accident."

He looked up at her. "Julianna, it was my son, his wife, and my grandchildren. We were having a family reunion."

He got up again and started pacing, wringing his hands. "It was over twenty years ago, and they were out on the boat. It was a beautiful day. Then the weather turned. The wind picked up, and it became dark. The weather report said a hurricane was coming. We yelled for them to come in, and they were trying to. Then something happened. The water got choppy, and the boat capsized. They started swimming towards shore. The wind was blowing so hard and there was hail, thunder and lightening. I ran down to the shore and out into the water. Then I heard it; it was a weird sound, like a bird or some animal chirping, a weird melody. My grandson screamed and said the lady wouldn't let go of his leg. Then he went under."

Julianna sat stunned as she watched Charles relive this terrible memory.

He went on. "My son dove down to help him but never came up. I started swimming and diving trying to find them, but they were gone. Five of them drowned that day."

He sobbed, and Julianna hugged him. "My son, my daughter in-law...Hayley was two, Charlie was nine, and Lily--" He broke down again. "She was only three months old."

He sat down in the rocking chair and just stared at her. "That's why my other children never come back here...They're afraid."

Julianna's knelt down beside Charles, trying to find the words to console him. Eric walked in and sat down on the foot stool. Julianna's mind wandered, thinking back about the video and Lady Lavonne and Emily and her…the lady under the water.

Her thoughts were cut short when Charles said, "Charlotte got mad at me a couple of nights ago and told me that right before Lady Lavonne died she'd confided in her. It was crazy. She said Lavonne told her some of the Wiccans from eons ago had cast a spell or something, and they were here now, and they would save us all." He laughed, then he grew very quiet again.

Julianna felt all of the blood drain from her face. She felt sick and lightheaded. It was true, but she couldn't tell him that. It was crazy. What was happening? Eric stood up and grabbed her to steady her. Everything was starting to make sense. The puzzle was coming together, but the picture it was making terrified her.

"Oh, God, Eric" she whispered. "I hope I'm wrong about this."

"What?" he asked.

They left Charles, and she took him out into the living room. Lauren followed them. She proceeded to pour her soul out to him and tell him everything—her dreams, the Hastings, how she thought it was the family from two hundred years ago, how they were still alive.

Eric's reaction was not what she'd expected. He became furious, ranting and raving. "How can you possibly be living in this fantasy world when one of your best friends has just died? What's wrong with you, Julianna? You've got to stop this. Your writing, it's…it's making you crazy. Right now, Charles needs us to be rational."

Julianna was stunned and hurt. Lauren couldn't believe her ears either. Julianna became hysterical and ran out of the room and up the stairs to the veranda. Through her tears, she looked up. Stars dotted the night's clear black sky. Why was Eric acting like this? He wasn't himself. Surely he of all people would know she would never make up such a story. Eric seemed different. He wasn't himself.

Lauren came up behind her when her phone indicated she had a text. She looked at her phone and gasped in horror.

"What?" Julianna inquired and grabbed her phone.

Julianna crumpled to the ground at what she saw on the screen.

"Julianna…I didn't frigging want you to see this…not now," Lauren sobbed.

"Who is sending you this?"

"I don't know the number. I don't recognize it, but look."

There were dozens of photos of Anya and Eric everywhere. Anya was in a skimpy black neglige, and they were lying on a bed in a passionate embrace, making out. Julianna let out a blood curdling scream.

"Bloody hell, Julianna, these are probably photo shopped. You can't believe that Eric would…"

Just then Eric ran up the stairs and saw the text. "Julianna you can't believe this. This never happened," he stuttered. His face turned red. "Julianna, I swear this never happened."

"Who would do this, then?" Julianna screamed. "Who would want to break us up…ruin our marriage?"

Lauren looked at the phone again and tapped her finger on the screen. "She bloody would."

Chapter 28

DOC walked down to the lake. He sat on a rock and looked down at his hands. He'd begun to age again; his hands were tired and worn. He couldn't stop trembling. He was frightened. What if his plan failed? He would let down all of mankind. Time was almost up. The Wiccans' spell would be broken, and the witches would gain their true forms again. Then no one would be safe. Everyone would die, and the world would cease to exist. Evil would claim it as its dominion, the bowels of Hell would rise up, and the devil would become one with his counterpart. Doc couldn't let that happen.

He wept as a soft breeze blew leaves down all around him. He looked at the base of the old oak tree, remembering how not too long ago he'd camouflaged the ground where he'd buried it. He looked at the sunset. The sky was a tranquil tangerine and fuchsia. A howl broke the silence. It took him back years ago to when everything began. The children were disappearing and everyone was so frightened. They had found body parts in a cave, then worse—mummified remains. No one knew who it was, who was doing these horrible things. Vigilante groups started searching people's houses. Then one night he saw them. He was riding home from a patient's cottage when his horse spooked and threw him. He thought he'd broken his leg, but since he'd touched the box, he healed quickly.

He crawled to the edge of the cliff and looked down at the lake. He heard clicking and chirping; he saw creatures crawling on their bellies out of the lake. They slithered onto the shore, long hair wrapped around their skeletal frames. They were inhuman and began screeching and snarling as they stood up. The moon glistened on their slimy bodies.

Then he heard chanting in the glen. It was Mrs. Erickson and the other Wiccan women. He ran to tell them of the danger and saw them holding hands around a bonfire, chanting. Then he saw the box. It was in the center, glowing. Screeches and screams from the lake made him look back, and he watched as the creatures turned into animals writhing in pain. Wolves, rats and, crows were what they'd become. And they started towards town. He remembered that was the same night of the big fire. The same night, he shuddered, when they tried to kill Mary.

Then his mind took him back further, before that terrible night. He was seated at the same exact place he was now, when a then eight-year-old Emily sat down beside him.

"Emily, you startled me," he laughingly said.

She looked at him. Her eyes rolled back in her head, turning them completely black. Her breathe stank of rotting sewage, and a demon's voice spoke.

"I'm not Emily. Emily is dead. I'm Hawah, and you will be my servant."

Doc was terrified. He thought at first maybe the trauma from her accident had caused this, damaged her brain. Then as quickly as she became Hawah, she changed back into Emily, the sweet, innocent little girl, with no recollection of what she'd just said.

"Doc, I wanted to thank you for saving me." She hugged him, then skipped off.

He sat stunned. What had she become?

It was at the debutante ball over two hundred years ago: the prophecy, the evil, the fire. Things didn't go as she'd planned. The killings stopped, and Emily went into hiding, taking Doc with her. Now she only had one more chance to get the prophecy right, one more chance to break the spell, this time as Anya. For him it was the beginning to an end. He must dig it up. He had successfully stolen it from the exhibit at the museum and hidden it from Anya.

His dreams had begun again, the same after that fateful night. Mary had come to him after she and her family disappeared and visited him in his sleep. She would grab his hand. She wouldn't speak but telepathically told him over and over again:

Three will save them
the rest shall rise
Protect the key
Safely hide.

What does it mean? How can I protect them from…from Anya. He needed their help. He knew they were still alive, but where? He'd helped them hide, brought them food in the cave. Then they just disappeared. They couldn't die. They were like him, forced to live for all eternity. If only he knew where they were. He needed them. He couldn't do it alone. It would be impossible. Mary was the chosen one, not him. He was just part of the plan to make everything right again, to stop the madness. The Wiccans had goodness and righteousness on their side. They cast the spell on the witches to change them. Without their true forms, they weren't as dangerous, but the witches had found a way around that. They couldn't travel far from the water, so they found underground streams to the ocean and spread their seed all over the world. Every night after their kills, they had to go back to the water. It was where they got their power, a portal to the underworld and Hawah.

The spell the Wiccans had cast was running out, and the witches were becoming more powerful, killing more people. Soon the spell would be broken, especially if Anya could recreate the events of that fateful night over two hundred years ago and undo what the Wiccans had done.

Chapter 29

THERE was no funeral, just a gathering of close friends and Charles' two remaining grown children: Charles Jr., his wife Elise, and their two teenage daughters, Audette and Paulette, then their youngest daughter Evelyn, her husband Aaron, and their three children, Andrew, Aden and Adam. They all stood on the veranda. The day was gray and dismal, as if the world knew someone extraordinary had died.

How could people go on about their day when someone so special is gone forever, Julianna thought. She struggled with the reality of never seeing Charlotte again, never seeing her sweet face or hearing her reassuring voice answering all of Julianna's relentless questions on life and love. Charlotte was the closest thing that Julianna had ever known of a mother. Her mother had died when she was a toddler, a freak accident. When she questioned her father about it, he was very evasive. He would always just tell her how much her mother loved her, then drop the subject. She barely remembered her, just memories from pictures in her photo album.

Her mind jolted back to reality as Lauren nudged her with her elbow. That was her cue to read the poem, a lovely piece she had written with Lauren's help. She looked around at everyone standing on the veranda. Everyone was sad. Charles stood in his gray pin-striped suit holding his beloved's remains in a cold, gold ceramic vase. How was this fair? Julianna choked back tears as she struggled through the reading.

Charlotte's children told funny anecdotes about their mother, both sad yet sweet. She was well-loved. No one would ever be able to take her place. They all cried and laughed, reminiscing about her wonderful life. Then Charles handed them envelopes, letters that Charlotte had written each of them and hidden in her nightstand drawer. She had known her time was quickly approaching and had left a list of who was to inherit precious heirlooms. Julianna was shocked when Charles handed her a small box.

"What's this?"

Charles cleared his throat. "Charlotte just found this...in the old chest in the attic. She was saving it for your birthday. She was so excited to give it to you. She said you'd understand why, whatever that means."

Julianna slowly opened the box. There was an old ring inside. Its silver was tarnished, but the stone was a beautiful, large greenish purple gem.

"An Alexandrite," she gasped.

"It changes colors," Charles explained.

"I know. It's beautiful. Thank you."

She stood up and hugged him tightly.

Julianna put the ring on her finger. It fit perfectly, and the stone began to change colors. She showed it to Eric, Lauren and her dad. Lauren insisted on examining it. She took her small magnifying glass out of her purse and put it to her eye, artfully examining every part of it.

"What's this?"

"What?" Julianna responded as she and Eric watched Lauren closely examining the ring.

"There are initials engraved…right here."

Julianna squinted, trying to see what she was talking about.

"M.H." Lauren exclaimed, looking at Julianna's stunned face.

***

Mr. Erickson knocked on the ramshackle cottage door. Mrs. Hastings opened it, surprised to find him standing there.

"Mr. Erickson, what a wonderful surprise…do come in."

"Thank you. Nice to see you again, Mrs. Hastings. May I please have the pleasure to speak to Ms. Mary?"

"Why yes, Mr. Erickson, please excuse me."

She went over to the bedroom and quietly knocked on the door, then disappeared through it. Soon she came back out with both Mary and Annabelle following closely behind.

"Hello, Mr. Erickson," they shyly said as they curtsied.

"Hello, Ladies." Then he looked at Mary. "Ms. Mary, I've brought you a present. My wife and I have extreme appreciation for everything you have done for Emily. If not for you…" His voice choked with emotion. "Well, we would have lost Emily."

Then he handed a tiny package wrapped in tissue paper to Mary. Mary sat at the small kitchen table and unwrapped it. It was the most beautiful ring Mary had ever seen. Its silver sparkled like the most brilliant star, and the stone was a breathtaking vision that constantly changed colors. She placed it on her finger as it continued to go from purple to green to blue to yellow-orange over and over again.

Mr Erickson stood staring at the ring. "I've never seen it do that before," he exclaimed. "It's an Alexandrite. I had your initials engraved inside. I hope you like it."

"I love it," she gasped and hugged him tightly.

Then he looked at Mrs. Hastings. "Mrs. Hastings, I have a business proposition I need to discuss with you."

"Yes?" Mrs. Hastings responded.

"Well I know you're without your husband, bless his soul, and with the events that have transpired over the last few weeks, my wife is with child and has fallen ill. She is unable to care for our family, unable to cook or clean. Do you suppose…" He adjusted his coat and looked pleadingly at her. "Could you find it in your heart to possibly fill a position as caretaker at Erickson manor? It would be cooking and cleaning, and I'd pay you handsomely. The girls are very responsible. Victoria will be a big help, and now that Emily is better…" His voice trailed off as he patiently waited for an answer.

"Oh, how kind of you, Mr. Erickson, but I couldn't possibly leave my children alone. They're not of age," Mrs. Hastings replied.

"Oh, Mrs. Hastings, not to worry. "We'd love to have you bring them along. My girls would enjoy playmates. I'm not just asking you, I'm begging you, Mrs. Hastings."

Mrs. Hastings looked around at her meager surroundings. It needed so much repair, and she couldn't possibly fix the cabin by herself.

"Oh, alright," she shyly accepted.

He noticed her gaze and offered to send some workmen to start fixing the cabin before the heavy rains came.

"Mr. Erickson, how can I refuse? Thank you." She gingerly shook his hand. It was the first time she had smiled in a very long time.

***

After the gathering on the veranda, Julianna and Eric went

back to their room adjacent from the Ericksons' mansion. Julianna sat quietly on the bed looking at the split ends on her hair, wondering whether she should get it cut and how short or just trimmed. Any thought was welcome except the realization her sweet friend was gone forever. Eric came over and rubbed her shoulders. It felt good, but then she remembered the pictures on the phone and pulled away.

"Jules, I need to talk to you."

"About what?" she snapped, bringing her knees up to her chin and wrapping her arms tightly around them as not to let the hurt in.

"I need to tell you the truth about the other night."

She glared at him, then covered her face and started crying. She didn't want to hear any more. She couldn't stand any more pain.

"No, I don't want to know," she sobbed.

"No, no, nothing happened." He gently wrapped his strong arms around her. "I love you, Julianna, only you. There's never been anyone else. Please believe me."

He began kissing her softly on her face and eyes, then lips. Then he stopped. She looked at him, her tear stained face waiting for an explanation.

"The other night, I was working at the office, and Anya called and asked if she could come by. She needed some help finding a property close to the Newlington Estate. She said she needed privacy, and her trailer was getting too cramped; she couldn't stay in the mansion because there was too much chaos. So I pulled up a listing, a house close by. It had just come on the market. The owners were relocating to Paris. He was a bigwig art dealer. Anyway she wanted to see it, so I took her there. It was all very innocent. On the way she offered me a new flavored power drink she was thinking of backing. It was good—tasted like a mocha coffee drink. Then when we got to the house, I started feeling strangely, and the next thing I remember, I was here in bed with you. I must have blacked out."

Julianna just stared at him. "So you're saying she drugged you and took those hideous pictures?"

"Yeah...I think that's what happened," he said sheepishly.

"I knew she couldn't be trusted, that BITCH!"

She threw the vase from the nightstand, smashing it against the wall. Julianna sobbed uncontrollably, hitting at Eric. He grabbed her wrists.

"Listen, I don't remember, Julianna. You have to believe me. I love you. I'd never do anything to hurt you, or our marriage. Anya gives me the creeps. She's...she's unnatural. She scares me."

The next day Eric and Julianna asked Lauren to look at the pictures of Eric and Anya once again. The two of them were on the bed in a passionate kiss. Eric's shirt was off and Anya was in a skimpy negligee. At a closer look, Eric looked like he was passed out.

"What a bitch," Lauren muttered, staring through the magnifying glass. "She set you up."

Eric nodded.

"I knew I didn't like her....Always trust first impressions," Julianna sternly said.

Eric was furious. "I'm going to confront her, and I don't care who's around. She's trying to ruin our life, our marriage... Why? She could have anybody. Why me?"

Julianna gasped. "Oh my God, Eric, it's like before." She looked at him, terror spreading though her body. You're her Stephen."

"What? That's crazy talk," he responded.

"No, it makes perfect sense," Lauren exclaimed. "We need to go to the Hastings, and Eric, you need to come with us."

Julianna knew Lauren was right.

Chapter 30

As they drove to the Hastings', Julianna's stomach was in knots. How would they react? She didn't want to scare them. Eric pulled up in front of the quaint house. Julianna thought it ironic that their house now was so similar to the cottage they had before.

How could all this be possible? What kind of anomaly was this? she pondered.

"Hello, Mrs. Hastings," Eric said as she opened the front door.

"Why hello, Mr. Hawthorn. It's so nice to see you again."

She looked at Julianna and Lauren as they stood awkwardly, not knowing what to do with their hands, then back at Eric "What brings you here?"

"Mrs. Hastings, I…we have some questions." He looked at Julianna. "I can't do…"

"Mrs. Hastings," Julianna continued.

"We need to ask you something. It might sound crazy."

"Please, come in," she said, looking troubled.

They sat on the sofa, and Julianna continued. "Have your relatives always lived here in Salem?"

"Yes," came an answer from the other room, and Mary walked in.

"Mary," her mother scolded.

187

"Mother, they already know."

She walked over to Julianna and knelt down, grasping her hands. She saw the ring and gasped, then looked deep into Julianna's eyes.

"It's you isn't it? Victoria, you've come back."

Mary's whisper stirred something deep within Julianna's memory. New memories of long ago began to surface to her conscious mind. Her brain had a jolt of electricity, of knowing, and she saw through new eyes, different eyes, not only hers but who she'd been before...Victoria Erickson.

"Mary," she gasped and hugged her tightly, then looked at her, touching her face and hair. "You're alright. You're alright." She began crying and hugging her again.

Eric and Lauren just sat, unable to speak. Julianna had transformed. Somehow she looked different. It was like she'd become someone else.

"Mary, I'm so sorry what happened to you that night. It was horrible. I tried to stop her." She began crying again.

"Victoria, I'm alright. Please stop crying." Mary sat beside her trying to console her. "What Emily didn't know is that she couldn't kill me. Her plan failed," Mary explained.

"Mary...Emily is Anya Thornsen, the actress. She's making a movie. It's called *The Angel Box*." Julianna explained.

"I know." Mary sighed. It was as if the weight of the world had just been put on her shoulders.

Just then Annabelle walked through the front door, surprised by their presence. She jumped and started laughing but quickly stopped when she noticed how solemn everyone was. "What's wrong?"

Mary stood up. "Julianna remembers who she was...before."

Annabelle looked at Mary, then at Julianna. It was as if she was seeing Julianna for the first time, only it was Victoria's soul that now was just making itself known. She couldn't believe her eyes.

"Victoria, is it you?" Annabelle gasped.

Julianna nodded her head.

"And look," Mary gestured to the ring.

Annabelle covered her mouth as did Mrs. Hastings who was just coming to grips with her daughter's discovery. Then Annabelle looked at Eric and Lauren. They looked totally astonished at what was transpiring.

She walked over to Eric. "And do you remember as well?"

Eric looked at Annabelle. "I don't know what you're talking about," he muttered.

Mary interrupted Annabelle. "Of course he doesn't. He was never touched by it, as far as we know."

"Did you touch the box?"

"No…not directly. I always had something over it or on my hands."

"Well, that is good, but it doesn't really matter. If it wants to connect with you, it could go through steel."

"So you're saying," Julianna asked, "it connected with me on purpose?"

"Yes," Mary answered. "For some reason it needed you to know the truth."

"And Eric," Mary said. "I know this is hard for you to believe, but you were Stephen back then, and for some reason the universe has brought both of you back together." She looked at them, then at her mother and sister.

Lauren was trying to understand the situation. She was used to dealing with logic and science. "So what you're saying is that the Angel Box has power…We knew that. So if you touch it, and it wants to connect with you, you…what?"

"You're immortal. You live forever," Mary stated.

Julianna gasped, "What? You mean I'm going to live forever?"

Mary grasped her hand. "It connected with you, right?

Julianna nodded as tears streamed down her face.

Mary went on. "And if you're healed by someone who connected with it, I guess reincarnation."

"Oh, that's the reason…" Julianna realized. "Doc Briggs was there in my first vision as Victoria; he must have healed me."

Lauren looked puzzled. "Does what's happening around the world—the rats and the plague, the weird behavior of the wolves and crows—have anything to do with it?" "In a way," Mary answered. "It's all connected."

"What about the lake?"

Lauren watched as Mary sat down and curled up in the fetal position, hugging her legs.

Annabelle whispered, "No."

"They need to know everything, Annie…everything that happened to me."

Annie reluctantly agreed and nodded her head.

"Julianna, you don't even know what happened after…" Mary swallowed hard. "After they burned me at the stake."

They all cringed, and Mrs. Hastings began sobbing.

Mary went on to tell of the fateful night that changed them forever:

"I was kidnapped from my house by a bunch of men with hoods covering their faces, even though the witch trials had been deemed unfair years earlier because the residents of

Salem called it an abomination to mankind. But then a new secret society of vigilantes formed and began kidnapping and murdering suspected witches. You see, children had started going missing again, dozens of children. Their parents were frantic; the fathers, brothers, and grandfathers decided to take matters into their own hands.

"The true witches kidnapped the children and took them into a cave. It was their coven. They would suck the very life from the children; it rejuvenated them and gave them unmeasurable powers, killing the poor children, leaving them mummified. The vigilantes found the coven and in the remains, they also found my ring. Someone had stolen it the night before and placed it there. They naturally thought I was one of them. That's when they kidnapped me and took me to the rose garden behind the mansion along with many others, all innocents. They tied us up to stakes high above on hay and kindling.

"I could hear the music and all the laughter from inside the mansion. I knew Mr. Erickson was inside and would help me if only I could get his attention. He would have saved me, but my screams for him were silenced when...when..."

Mary started crying. Her mother and sister gently hugged her and stroked her hair. "Those bastards." Mrs. Hasting tried to choke back her tears. "They cut out her tongue."

Eric, Julianna and Lauren gasped and sat stunned.

Mary went on. "They set the brush on fire."

"They still had their hoods on so no one would know who they were," Ann explained.

Mrs. Hastings was crying. It was too much for her to relive. "Someone threw a brick," she sobbed, "through the mansion's window, a paper with the names of the victims wrapped around it."

"I remember," Julianna whispered. "The brick almost hit father. He ran outside. The smoke and the blaze were huge. Everyone from the ball ran outside, all those people screaming, on fire." She began sobbing as Eric wrapped his arms around her. "We didn't know what was happening or who they were... then my father read Mary's name. He went crazy trying to put out the fire, but he didn't know which one you were. Then the fire grew larger, and wind starting blowing. It caught the east side of the mansion on fire. Everyone was running for their lives. Everyone, except Emily. She just stood staring at the fire with a smug smile on her face. I knew then she truly was evil. Something dark lived inside of her."

Julianna shook her head and looked at the floor. Her hands were trembling.

Mary looked sadly at her. "It still does, Julianna. She won't rest until she gets her revenge against you. She needs Eric to fall in love with her so she can break the spell. She'll have unlimited powers and will remain beautiful forever." Eric shuddered, and Mary went on. "But there's more. The lake is the portal for all eternity so the evil can escape. The curse that Mother and the other Wiccan women put on the witches will be broken, and their true forms will be revealed. The world will manifest into a new reality. Mankind will cease to exist, and the demons will extract the energy from every living thing, making it literally hell on Earth."

"We can't let that happen," Julianna gasped.

"I will never let that happen," Eric angrily screamed.

Mary shook her head. "Her power is growing. Her magic is unimaginable, but she needs one more thing."

"The Angel Box, she must have it. It's the piece of the

puzzle she doesn't have yet. It's her answer to everything, and it's still missing," Annabelle replied.

Mary looked at her. "I need to find someone who I believe knows where it is."

"Who?" Julianna questioned.

"Doc," Mary replied.

"You mean Anya's doctor friend?"

"He's not her friend," Mary explained. "He's trapped. We need to find him and talk to him."

Julianna thought it would be a good idea to take her father along since he'd actually seen the box before and could tell if it was authentic.

"We can't go with you," Mary said.

"It's too dangerous. You need to bring Doc back here so we can figure things out," Julianna agreed, "but where do you think he'd be?"

"Probably with Anya. She's keeping him close," Mary sighed.

Chapter 31

JULIANNA, Lauren, and Eric got in the SUV and started towards the mansion. Julianna looked at both of them solemnly. "How am I supposed to face her and pretend nothing has happened."

"Listen, Jules, she's evil. You have to try," Lauren said.

They first went to the Ericksons' and picked up Julianna's dad. They tried to explain the bizarre predicament to him as he looked at them in disbelief.

"There have been many odd and strange things that I've witnessed in my life, more than most I'd say. Probably comes with the occupation of unearthing things that maybe should have stayed buried. I've seen spirits, and I've heard weird noises, terrifying noises, many things that can't be explained. I've never talked about it. I thought people would think I was insane. Now what you're telling me sounds unimaginable. Nice to know there's someone else out there just as crazy as me." Then he chuckled.

"We need to go to the movie set," Lauren said. "Now." She looked at her watch. "They'll be taking their lunch break soon. Blimey, it's almost noon."

"Okay, but I'm going to stay in the car. I'm not an actor, and I never want to see that bitch again," Eric blurted.

"It's okay, honey. I understand." Julianna was shaking as she kissed him.

He pulled up to one of the large trucks with a boom on it parked adjacent to the set. They jumped out of the SUV and started walking towards the mansion. It was bustling with activity. Stagehands carried large props; actors and actresses darted in and out in their elaborate method costumes. And then they saw her. Anya was wearing a pastel pink silk robe which cascaded down her voluptuous frame. She was more beautiful than ever, her hair hanging in soft curls down to her waist. She was talking to a man. His back was to them, but she seemed upset, angrily whispering to him. Her demeanor quickly changed as she spotted them walking towards her.

As Anya made eye contact with Julianna, a strange look, a smug smile spread across her face. Perhaps she was waiting for a reaction to the scandalous pictures that had been sent. When there was no reaction, she seemed disoriented, then annoyed. "Hello, Anya," Julianna cheerily said.

Anya was flustered and speechless. Julianna exuded kindness.

Who's the actress now, she thought to herself as she delivered an Academy Award performance. Introducing her father to Anya, Professor Hilard played along, taking her hand and kissing it.

"My dear, you're lovelier in person than you are on the silver screen."

He oozed charm, and Julianna and Lauren played right along with him. The man Anya had been talking to turned around.

"You do remember Doctor Swenson, don't you, Julianna?"

She waited to see a reaction. "You remember, after that dreadful fall."

Julianna remained poised, even though every experience seemed different because of her newfound memories.

"Of course, Dr. Swenson. How nice to see you again. Still in the states visiting?"

He noticed the difference, too. She could tell by his expression which she hoped only she had noticed.

"Uh...yes. Yes," he answered.

"He'll be here till the end," Anya said solemnly.

"And how long will that be," Professor Hilard asked.

Anya looked at Doc. "That depends," she said, staring at the Doctor. He nervously started adjusting his cuff-links. "Probably a week or two if everything goes accordingly." Then she laughed a strange, bizarre laugh.

Suddenly Anya noticed some stage hands sneaking a cigarette under the large oak tree adjacent from the rose garden. She excused herself and darted over to reprimand them.

Julianna quickly took the opening. "Dr. Swenson, we have an urgent message for you," she whispered.

He looked confused and wondered who it could be from. *Who could they know who could possibly know me*, he thought.

Julianna quickly slipped him the note. "Don't let Anya see," she warned.

He glanced at it suspiciously. "Mary Hastings" was printed in red writing on the scrap of paper. He gasped, then looked confused. "But how...where?"

It was as if Anya knew. She quickly whirled around and stared at them. Julianna's dad sensed this and slapped Doc on his back and started laughing. Dr. Swenson quickly put the note in the breast pocket of his jacket as Anya walked back over to them.

"What's so funny?" she asked.

Julianna fabricated an explanation about her father attending a seminar on "Sociology in the workplace."

"It was many years ago, and amazingly, it was Dr. Swenson who gave it," she lied.

Anya looked at the doctor suspiciously. "Since when do you give lectures on sociology?"

"Anya, I have many interests and degrees in many different fields. You know that," he chuckled.

Anya knew that was a true statement, so she turned to Professor Hilard. "And what exactly is your profession?"

"I'm an ar--"

Julianna quickly interrupted. "He's an art historian...yep, his entire life."

Anya eyed them both suspiciously. "Really."

Then she turned back to look for any more of the stage hands meandering around. She was in a dreadful mood and needed to scream at someone, but the oak tree was void of smokers as she quickly stocked off.

They all let off a sigh of relief as beads of sweat trickled down Doc's forehead. He wiped it off with a handkerchief. They watched as Anya quickly walked into the mansion, and they ran to the SUV and helped Doc in.

"Eric, you remember Doc?"

Eric nodded and grasped his hand. Electricity jolted them both as memories stirred between them. Eric remembered Doc taking him on horse back to his small cottage and nursing him back to health. Eric gasped.

Doc looked deep into his eyes. "Stephen, is that you?"

Eric felt himself slipping back. His soul was leaving his body and was falling rapidly back, back to the past, to his memories, but it wasn't memories. He was there. He awoke to a dim light, flickering candles. It was chilly. He pulled the soft patchwork quilt tightly up towards his chin as he saw his breath puff out in small clouds around his face. He heard the crackling of a fire and footsteps as a man put more wood on it. The wind and rain were whipping outside. He could see it through the crude window. The man took his coat off and warmed his hands by the fire, then stirred the thick soup that was in the cast iron pot teetering above it. Doc Briggs turned around and saw Stephen.

"So you've decided to rejoin the living, I see," he chuckled.

Stephen sat up and rubbed his head. It throbbed wildly.

"Here's something for the pain."

Doc handed him a small white pill. He gladly gulped it down with a cup of water.

"What happened? Why am I here?"

He looked around, bewildered. He was lying on a small bed.

"You don't remember?" Doc asked.

"No, one minute I was eating dinner with Victoria and her family, and then..." His face turned white. "Emily. Did I? Why was I kissing Emily?"

"I don't know," Dr. Briggs sighed.

The shock of that memory transported him back to the present, and he jolted in his seat. Dr. Swenson and Eric sat stunned.

"Are you alright?" Julianna asked.

Eric was sweating profusely as he shook his head. "We

need to leave," he muttered and stepped on the gas, heading towards the Hastings.

The streets were abandoned as they drove to the Hastings', all except for crows that were perched everywhere, as far as the eye could see. The crows watched them drive past as they sat on the fence posts, telephone wires, trees and buildings, their beady eyes following the car's every move. The crows watched them drive into the Hastings' driveway. The crows were sitting on the railings as they made their way up the front porch.

"Why are they watching us?" Julianna whispered.

"They're going to let Anya know," Doc answered. He grabbed the railing as he climbed up the steps to the Hastings' house, and one of the crows tried to peck his hand. He jerked it back. "Try to stay calm and don't antagonize them," he whispered.

Mary opened the door and gasped as she saw the crows. "Quick, get in here," she said as she closed the door. She hugged Doc. "I'm so glad to see you," she said, choking back tears.

Doc was emotional as well as the Hastings women all hugged him affectionately.

"They know what we're about to do. We have to figure this out quickly before Anya finds out," Mary explained.

Doc looked at her sympathetically. "Mary, her power has grown. What she is attempting to do is unimaginable." He grabbed her hands and gazed into her eyes. "We must stop her," he sighed, "but I'm not sure how."

Mrs. Hastings had iced tea waiting for them, ironically in glasses etched with little birds. They all nervously laughed. Eric was still sweating profusely. Julianna went to the kitchen and rinsed a towel with cool water to apply to the back of his neck.

"Eric, what's wrong," Annabelle asked.

He laughed nervously. "I don't really know. When I shook Doc's hand, something happened; I went somewhere else."

"To a different time?" Doc asked.

"Yes." Eric looked puzzled. "How did you know?"

Doc stroked his beard. "I don't know. I just felt your soul was gone for a split second. I've done a lot of research on quantum physics, time travel. Here, let me show you." He took a napkin and wrinkled it. "Pretend that the cloth is time. Now when it's wrinkled, that's when it becomes an anomaly, if it touches another piece of the cloth or curves or folds. Time can bleed, as you will, into another, putting the theory forward that time travel is possible and has been happening for centuries. My theory goes much further. Take an accordion; it's pleated, and when you compress it, the pleats fold over onto itself, sometimes touching. When that happens, time is bound to repeat itself such as what is happening now. But sometimes it rips. That is the worst scenario, for if that happens, the entire time continuum is jeopardized and the wormholes which time travels through become a black hole that implodes onto itself making our time, our reality vanish forever."

Everyone sat stunned, silently trying to understand what Doc was telling them. He went on. "What Anya is trying to do is end our world and make her vision a reality, literally hell on earth. It's not a rip, but it's a horrible outcome nonetheless."

Mary looked at him and spoke in a hushed tone, looking out at the crows perched on their house. "I realize the Angel Box is important to stop this, but why?"

"I don't have all the answers. I just know it's a powerful entity from God. She wants it, and she can't continue without it," he answered.

Chapter 32

ANNABELLE helped Mary walk back to their cottage. Mary was limping and badly bruised by Emily's attack, but more than that, her spirit was crushed by Emily's verbal brutality. She had thought of Emily as a sister. Now she didn't know who or what Emily had become.

Mother had told them never to go past the old cave, but it was a short cut and Annabelle wanted to get Mary home as quickly as possible. The sun was setting and night would soon be upon them.

That's when then the danger came.

Children were missing, being taken, and no one knew who the culprits were. At night they would hear strange noises, screeches, unearthly sounds that sent chills down their spines. Often they would end up in bed with Mother huddling close together till dawn when it would stop.

Mary's nose was bleeding, and her eyes were starting to swell shut. Annabelle saw the cave and started walking quickly past it, when they heard a strange whistling, then chirping. The wind started blowing, and the tree branches bent wildly in the breeze. The strange sounds grew louder. It was coming from the cave.

Annabelle's curiosity got the best of her. "Mary, stay right here. I'll be right back." She quickly walked towards the cave's opening. Her heart beat wildly in her chest. She looked back at Mary, who huddled under a fir tree, then she ducked down and entered the small opening of the cave. It was dark, and she made her way by feeling the dank walls as she carefully crept deep into the bowels of the earth. All the while the strange clicking and chirping was getting louder, but now she heard something else. She heard whimpering, crying children.

Children. Children are down there, she thought.

Terror filled her heart as the whimpering and crying grew louder. Soon she saw a glow; it was a fire. She hid behind a boulder and watched as creatures with long matted hair slithered around the fire. They were unclothed but seemed to be neither male or female. Their hair was long and dark, matted against their skeletal frames. They were bent over and had large hollow eyes that glowed a greenish color. Their skin was transparent gray, and their features were sharp and inhuman. They would put their heads back and let out the chirping and clicking sounds. She watched as they took the small children and sucked their souls from them. The children struggled, then grew stiff and became mummified. Then the creatures tossed their small bodies in a pile. She had to quickly covered her mouth to muffle her sobs, tears stinging her eyes. The remaining children were so dehydrated and malnourished they were too weak to run or put up a fight. There was nothing Annabelle could do to help them. The creatures soon began to purge the children's souls out.

Then Annabelle saw it the Angel Box. It was glowing, and the souls of the poor children evaporated into it. The creatures grew in size, becoming more human-like, more female. The more they sucked the souls from the children, the more beautiful they became.

The souls kept being purged from the creatures, and the Angel box glowed with the radiance of the sun. It blinded her. She covered her eyes against the intense light. Then she quietly made her way out of the cave and was so traumatized that she forgot all that she'd seen, burying the terror deep inside.

***

Annabelle gasped. "I know why."

Slowly she recanted what she remembered. Sorrowfully, she relived that terrible night as everyone sat terrified by its staggering reality.

"I've seen them too," Dr. Swenson admitted. "They came out of the lake. They weren't human. The evil in the lake needs the Angel Box."

"But why?" Julianna asked.

"There are portals. The Angel Box energy is drawn to them. The more children those hideous creatures killed made them more powerful, but the Angel Box also became stronger. You see, the children's souls, a large portion of it is connected to energy. The pure and good energy, that's what the Angel Box keeps inside, what it absorbs. It's much more powerful than the witches."

Professor Hilard nodded his head. "It makes sense now, why the Angel Box disappears wherever it is. If a portal is near, the box goes to it."

"Exactly," Doc Swenson responded. "The portals—they move around, most of them anyway. I've tried to figure it out, but every time I think I've found one, I hit a dead end."

"I don't understand. Why is Anya so urgent to have the Angel Box," Julianna sighed.

Doc Swenson's face grew grim. "She has to reenact what

happened on that fateful night…the night of the debutante ball. She needs to free the remaining energy from the Angel Box to open the portal to the underworld for the devil's daughter."

They all gasped.

"But there's more." He looked at Eric. "She needs love. Love is the most powerful energy. To ensure it works, she wants you, Eric."

Julianna burst into tears, and Eric turned gray.

"You've got to be kidding, Doc. This is ridiculous," Eric yelled.

"No, I'm very serious. This has been planned for hundreds of years. The first time she failed. She can't fail again. If she succeeds, our world, our very souls will be lost forever."

"We can't let that happen," insisted Professor Hilard. "We need to find the Angel box and keep it from her."

Just then the crows outside began to caw so loudly everyone had to cover their ears. The birds went into a frenzy, breaking windows and pecking at the door wildly, their beaks shredding the door as Doc and the rest of them stacked tables up against it. The girls screamed, all except Mary who remained stoic as if in a trance. Then in an instant, with a rush of their wings, the crows were gone.

Annabelle stood up. "Do you suppose they understood us, what we intend to do?"

Mary nodded her head.

"They're going to tell Anya," Dr. Swenson murmured.

"We need to find the Angel Box before she does," Professor Hilard replied.

Mary looked at Doc Swenson. "Take them," she solemnly stated.

He nodded and gathered the men.

"Eric, I want to go with you," Julianna cried.

"No, sweetie, you stay here. It'll be alright."

Eric kissed and hugged her tightly. She didn't want to let go. What if he never came back…What if none of them came back? How could she bear to go on living!

Julianna looked at the broken windows, at the devastation the crows had left behind. The destruction was just at the Hastings'. Neighbors were walking by staring at their house. Some passersby were taking pictures with their phones.

"Please stay here," Professor Hilard pleaded.

"We'll be back soon. I know where it is," Doc Swenson whispered.

As they left, Eric handed a business card to Mrs. Hastings. "He's my handyman. Call him. Tell him I said it's an emergency."

She nodded her head. "Thank you," she responded.

"Other than him, don't open the door for anyone else," Eric said sternly.

They all nodded.

Julianna hugged her dad. "Be careful," she whispered.

The last thing Eric saw of his beautiful wife, she was standing on the front porch, tears streaming down her face. She blew a kiss and waved goodbye.

Chapter 33

MRS. Hastings called the number on the card Eric had given her. The repairman agreed to come over immediately with a new door and panes of glass.

"What did you say happened again?" he inquired.

"A crow attack," Mrs. Hastings explained.

"Well now, that's a new one," he chuckled. "I'll be there shortly."

Within ten minutes, there was a knock on the door. Mary looked out the shattered window. There was a van with "Marvin's Custom Home Repair Service" printed in colorful letters on the side.

"Wow, that was blooming fast," Lauren nervously laughed. Mrs. Hastings opened the door, and that was the last thing they remembered.

***

"When did you take the Angel Box?" Eric asked Doc.

"About two weeks ago. It was at the Salem museum. I broke in, dismantled the security systems, video cameras, et cetera, and took it. It was simple," he went on. "I buried it under the old oak tree by the lake."

"By the Ericksons'?" Professor Hilard inquired.

"No, the other side. In the park," he replied. "We need to

wait till dark; we don't want anyone to see what we're doing. Anya has spies everywhere. When I took the box, something strange happened. Instead of a glow, it emitted a purple hue. There were numbers reflecting on the museums walls," Doc explained.

"What numbers?" Eric asked.

"It looked like a longitude and latitude. Do you have a map, Eric?"

"Yes, in the glove compartment."

Doc took the map out and opened it up.

"Just as I thought, it's in the old cave."

"What is?" Eric asked.

"I think a portal, a doorway to another time," Doc responded.

Eric turned onto the road going across the lake where they drove across the old wood covered bridge. It had been standing for more then two hundred years. There were dozens of people playing Frisbee with their dogs and numerous family picnics at the park. Bright, colorful kites danced and twirled in the clear blue sky as children below squealed with delight. The playground was full of children and parents on the swing sets and large colorful slides.

Doc sighed. "They have no idea what the future holds for them if we don't succeed."

"Then we just have to make this work," Eric emphatically stated.

***

Julianna's head throbbed as she began to gain consciousness. *What happened*, she thought, trying to sit up.

She squinted her eyes, trying to see. It was dark and dank.

She smelled dirt beneath her. As her eyes grew accustomed, she was able to see a little. Flickering tourches lined the mason walls outside her cell. She felt a presence but couldn't see anything in the dark corner of her small cell. She crawled over to the bars, grasping them. They were rusted and cold. Outside the cell was a dim corridor, and she could make out other cells lining either side.

"Help." Her voice was hoarse and raspy; she needed water.

"Julianna?" She heard a whisper from the next cell.

"Lauren?"

She crawled closer to the wall and saw Lauren's hand reach around the corner through the bars. She grasped it and started sobbing. "What the hell happened?"

"It was Anya's people. They have us locked in the dungeon below the mansion," Lauren whispered.

"All of this is really true then, isn't it?" Julianna sobbed, trying to gain her composure. "Where are Annabelle, Mary, and Mrs. Hastings?"

"I don't know. They knocked us out with formaldehyde. I don't know where they put them." Then Lauren broke down.

"We need to find a way out of here," Julianna whispered.

"You think!" Lauren sarcastically replied back.

Just then the air in Julianna's cell grew thick, and the hairs on her neck stood up. There was a presence by her again, then a whisper, hot breath on her neck.

"You'll never get out of here alive."

She smelled rotted flesh. She screamed and scooted closer to the rusted bars. Julianna turned, trying to see in the darkness, but to no avail.

"Julianna, what happened?" Lauren screamed.

"Something's in here with me," Julianna gasped.

Once again she felt the breath on her neck and smelled the sickening stench.

"No!" she screamed.

***

The three men sat looking at the map as they rested under the oak tree. Eric kept texting Julianna, but she didn't respond. When he called her cell, it went directly to voice mail.

"I wonder what's going on?"

"She probably has a dead battery," Professor Hilard replied.

Knowing Julianna, that probably was true. Still, Eric felt uneasy. Soon the sunset came, and the warm day was turning into a chilly night as they watched the cars' lights slowly go over the bridge to the other side of the lake and back into town.

They went to the SUV and pulled shovels out of the back. Doc instructed them on where to dig, and soon the shovels hit the wood box Doc had buried the Angel Box in. "Wait, let me." Doc said. "I've already touched it. You can't, or you'll..." he paused.

"End up like you?" Professor Hilard replied.

"Exactly," he sighed.

He jumped down into the hole, started unearthing the wooden box with his hands, and opened up the top. The Angel Box began glowing inside. He grasped it, and the light went up his arms, quickly enveloping his entire body. He groaned in agony as the light surged through his body, changing his molecular age to a much younger version. His entire body wracked in pain as he writhed on the bottom of the hole.

Eric and Professor Hilard were helpless to do anything except watch in horror. When it ended, Doc was exhausted as he climbed out of the hole with the Angel Box. He stood up and brushed himself off.

"I never will get used to that," he moaned.

He was young and virile, not the elderly gentleman he used to be. He stood up straight, no longer bent over, and his hair had returned to a dark brown, no gray in sight. He seemed to be about 35 years old. He looked at Eric and Professor Hilard.

"That was a strong one," he groaned.

They were in shock, speechless.

Doc looked at them and laughed. "Hurry we need to fill up this hole and get out of here."

"Not so fast," a voice came from behind them.

They whirled around as Anya stepped out from behind a tree, her entourage standing behind her.

"Anya, I was just about to bring this to you," he quickly stated.

"Sure you were." She eyed the other men, and her henchmen drew guns.

"Doc, you always were a good conman, but you forgot I'm much better," she laughed as she walked up closer to him. "I see you've rejuvenated."

She looked him up and down, then licked him with her long, slimy tongue, much like a serpent. He pulled back as her henchmen grabbed him. Anya laughed a maniacal laugh, then looked at Professor Hilard. She walked up to him and grabbed his face.

"You lied to me. You're that famous archeologist, the one who wrote the book about the Angel Box."

She then pushed him down. Doc and Eric looked puzzled.

"Oh you didn't know. Maybe that's because it never got published. Somehow it mysteriously disappeared, and all the transcripts were lost…Pity." She smiled. "Then there was the unfortunate account at the airport where you were caught trying to smuggle the Angel Box out of the country."

Professor Hilard stood up. "You were behind that?"

Anya gasped. "Me? Oh, how can you blame little ol' me? You're the thief. You went to prison for two years, and lied to your wife and daughter about it, saying you were on a dig in Peru, leaving your wife and daughter alone, all alone." Anya paused and walked up to him again. "And your poor wife met with such an unfortunate accident."

Then Anya started laughing. Professor Hilard lunged at her, enraged, only to be hit from behind with the butt of a gun. He crumpled to the ground, unconscious. Eric lunged at her, and she raised her hands. Energy erupted from them, knocking Eric thirty feet into the air. He landed hard, breaking a rib.

Anya was upset. She didn't want to hurt Eric. Of all people, she loved him, but he startled her. She ran to him and stroked his head. "Eric I'm sorry."

He was unconscious.

"Take them to the mansion," she ordered, "and put them with the others, except for him."

She stroked Eric's hair, then kissed him. She turned and walked to the Angel Box. She ordered one of her men to retrieve it. He picked it up, but it remained dormant. Then she got into her limousine and sped off.

***

Julianna bolted backwards. Her heart was pounding, and she couldn't breathe. She heard something and felt the presence again. She saw something move in the darkest corner of her cell. She jumped as an entity scurried towards her on hands and knees. She screamed.

Lauren was frantic in her cell, unable to help her.

In the dim light Julianna saw a being, its long hair hanging down in front of its face. Julianna closed her eyes, expecting the worse. Nothing happened, only a whimpering. It sounded like a young child. She opened her eyes to see a young girl badly battered and bruised.

"Who are you?" Julianna whispered.

"I don't remember," the young girl sobbed.

Lauren was on the other side listening intently.

"Have you been here long?"

"I do believe it's been more than seven fortnights."

"Where do you come from?" Julianna continued.

"The last thing I remember is I was with my friends. We were berry picking in the glen. Then we heard some strange noises. We went--"

Then she gasped and started crying.

"What?" Julianna asked.

The little girl got in her lap and hugged her tightly. The stench almost made Julianna vomit.

"What's going on? Who's bloody in there?" Lauren asked.

"A little girl," Julianna replied.

The little girl was about seven or eight years old.

Julianna tried to console her. "Where do you live?"

"By the lake. My mother is a housekeeper at the Ericksons'."

"Wait...What?"

Julianna stared at the young girl's face through the dim light. She recognized the little girl. She was the one in the road and in the Ericksons' bedroom.

Chapter 34

ANYA was with her sound crew in the ballroom while the orchestra was warming up. Anya walked over to another one of her henchmen, giving him instructions, and he immediately went outside to make sure everything was ready for the scene they were going to shoot that night.

It must be exactly the same, she thought to herself. *This time she won't get away. Her soul, her energy will unlock it, and the energy will cause a shift in the axes, and the portal will open.*

A voice inside her spoke, reassuring her. "Yes, Anya, you need this, my princess. We've waited too long. Our dominion will become this reality, and the world that we have now will cease to exist. Our power will be unimaginable. Anything we want or desire will be ours for the taking with just a thought."

She smiled and combed her long blonde hair as she stared at her reflection in the ballrooms mirror. She grew more beautiful with every passing day as the evil inside her grew stronger.

***

"So you were kidnapped?"

"Yes, men took us to the witches. They were in a cave, and they..." She started crying. "They killed them," she whispered.

Julianna's mind raced. She remembered the story Annabelle

had told them. Was this real? Had this little girl been there? How was it possible?

"I escaped. I ran further into the cave, and there was a dead end. The witches were about to get me when something happened. I fell through and was on the outside, but the men found me again and brought me here.

"Does Anya know you're here?" Julianna asked.

"Who's Anya?" the little girl asked.

"She's the actress, tall, blonde hair."

"Oh, yes, her. She's the evil one. She told them to bring me down here. Why would she do that?"

Her big brown eyes stared up at Julianna.

"You're right, she is evil. What's your name?"

"Kathleen Elizabeth Thornton," the little girl whispered, "but everyone calls me Yesie."

"What year do you think it is Yesie?"

Yesie looked at Julianna strangely. "Well, 1792, the year of our Lord."

Julianna gasped.

All the while Lauren had been listening. "Jules, you have to tell her."

"Who's that?" Yesie asked.

"My friend, Lauren. Listen, Yesie, something strange and unimaginable has happened to you, and I know it's going to be hard to believe, but you're not in the year 1792 any longer."

"I'm not?" She stared at Julianna with wide eyes.

"No, I'm afraid your--"

A blood curdling scream cut through the darkness like a sharp knife. It was Mrs. Hastings.

Lauren started screaming. "Mrs. Hasting where are you?"

Then a heavy door slammed, and there was silence. The

little girl clung to Julianna, silently sobbing and shivering. She couldn't bring herself to tell the girl the truth. It was just too terrifying. She wanted to protect her. She'd been through too much already.

***

The men were taken back to the mansion and thrown into different cells in the dungeon, as Lauren and Julianna watched in horror. Eric was placed adjacent from Julianna's cell. She could barely make out his crumpled body lying on the cold dirt floor.

Please, God, let him be all right, she prayed to herself.

The little girl Yesie clung to her. Eric began to moan, writhing with pain.

"Eric are you okay?" Julianna sobbed.

All Eric could do was groan as he began to gain conscious. Every move he made, pain shot through him. He groaned as he felt where his rib was broken.

"Eric, Eric, are you okay?" Julianna whispered.

"No," he groaned. "My rib."

He gasped for air. The bone was jabbing into his lung. He knew he wouldn't last much longer.

"Eric," Doc whispered. "Can you crawl over here? I can help you."

He was about ten feet away, but the condition Eric was in, it might as well have been ten miles.

"Please, Eric, try. I can help you," Doc pleaded.

Eric tried to crawl but felt the bone jabbing into his lung. The only way was to stand up. He grasped the bars and hoisted himself up. The pain was severe, but he knew if he didn't do this, he would die. He grabbed the bars and shuffled his feet over to Doc. When he finally reached Doc, he was sweating profusely. Doc placed his hands through the bars over the broken rib. Eric felt the heat enter his body, and then he heard a click as the bone repaired itself and the pain subsided. Then he collapsed onto the cell's dirt floor.

"Thank God," Eric murmured. "I'm okay."

Julianna silently cried as she clung on to Yesie. How were they ever to get out of this? She had to try, with every inch of her being, figure a way...a solution to an immeasurable situation. She heard Mrs. Hastings scream again. She had to help them. She knew that Mrs. Hastings and the girls would survive; they had touched the box. But how long did its effects last? It had been more than two hundred years ago. Did the box's effects last forever? No one knew that answer.

She heard the large metal door open and close again, then heavy footsteps. It sounded like an army was approaching. Soon her worst fears were about to come true. Yesie started shaking and whimpering as Julianna moved into the darkest corner of the cell. The men—ten in all—stopped in front of her cell. She cringed as she heard the key turn in its rusted lock and closed her eyes as she heard the door creak open. The heavy footsteps loomed closer as she hid her head, clinging to Yesie. Then in an instant she felt her arm almost jerked out of its socket. Yesie was ripped from her, thrown across the cell, hitting the wall with a hollow thud. Yesie screamed but then was silent. Had they killed her?

She tried to see if Yesie was all right, but the men jerked her head around and placed a burlap sack over it. The men dragged Julianna kicking and screaming down the dirt corridor. The others could do nothing as they helplessly watched them take her through the metal door. Eric screamed at them to let

her go, but they paid no attention. The door slammed shut...
then silence.

Chapter 35

ANYA sat in her bedroom in front of her vanity. She looked at her reflection. Her long golden hair lay in soft curls as she brushed it repeatedly. She was growing more agitated and felt disconnected. She felt so different from the reflection she saw in the mirror. Her inner voice was hypnotic, telling her what she must do next. Somehow what used to be one entity inside her was separating. Did the entity inside her know this was happening? She was frightened. Would it suck her back in to its evil? For the first time in her long life, she felt regret, but it couldn't know. She had to repress her feelings. What would happen to her if it...if she found out? Would it kill her? Had enough time passed that the entity inside was losing its hold on her? Would she ever be herself again? Then as if it heard her thoughts, she was sucked back in, into evil. There was just one again, one entity. Emily had disappeared once again into Anya, once more into the devil's daughter, where only evil resided.

A knock on her door brought her out of her trance.

"What is it?" she screamed as she quickly walked to the door and opened it.

Mary was standing in front of her as a guard held her arms from behind.

"Well, what do we have here?" Anya smugly said, standing

in the doorway, her long silver silk robe draped over her supple frame shimmering in the dim candlelight.

"I've come to do as you ask," Mary stated, her voice firm and strong.

Anya eyed her up and down, annoyed she wasn't able to break her spirit.

"So you couldn't stomach your family being tortured."

She grabbed Mary's face and squeezed it tightly, bruising her. "Of course you couldn't. You're so good and pure."

Just touching Mary made her sick.

"You'd risk your own life for what? Them? Why?" Then Anya laughed.

She raised her hands, and Mary levitated and was thrown across the room into an adjacent wall where she crumpled and fell to the ground. Anya stormed over to her and lifted her up by her neck.

"The Angel Box will use up all its power soon, and you, my dear..." She looked deep into Mary's eyes. "You will die."

Then Anya threw her head back and laughed, still choking Mary by the throat. As Mary struggled for breath, Anya looked back at her, and it wasn't Anya's face. Mary gasped. It was the lady from the lake, the Devil's Daughter.

"And I will be free," a demonic voice whispered.

Then she dropped Mary, choking and sputtering on the floor. The guard was instructed to take her back to her cell. As Mary was dragged and thrown back into her small cage, she thought to herself, *You have no idea what you're up against Anya. You have no idea.*

***

For hours Julianna lay knocked unconscious in a laboratory.

She'd been placed on a sterile metal table, her hands and feet shackled. As she came to she could hear something in the next room. It was Mary. She listened intently. Mary was agreeing to something.

No, she thought. *What is happening? Anya can't have her way.*

She looked around the dimly lit room. There were stainless steel cabinets lining the walls stacked with jars. She assumed formaldehyde was in them preserving whatever disgusting things were inside. She squinted her eyes and stared at one particularly big jar with something large floating inside. She heard the metal door slam and the jars shook, their contents moving. Inside the murky liquid a mass turned. She screamed in terror as a face with a grimace turned towards her. It was Lady Lavonne's head.

She realized all of the jars had different body parts in them. She screamed again and struggled to get free. Trying to pry her hands and feet from the tight shackles only made deeper gashes in her skin.

Anya's guards quickly entered the laboratory where Julianna lay, their faces void of emotion. Julianna had never noticed this before. It was as if they weren't human but merely puppets that Anya controlled. Then she recognized one of them. She gasped. It was the sergeant she'd talked to at the police station. What was happening? Did Anya control everyone? They were clearly under Anya's spell. Who could she get to help them now?

The sergeant and other guards dragged her back to her cell where Yesie sat battered and bloody in the darkest corner.

Why did they take me to that room? she thought as Yesie climbed back into her lap, sobbing uncontrollably.

"Are you alright, Yesie?"

The little girl nodded, and Julianna carefully hugged her.

There must be a reason, she pondered. *They didn't do anything to me.*

"Julianna, are you alright?" Lauren whispered.

"Yes, I'm fine...I think they were just trying to scare me."

Lauren listened intently. "Julianna, when they brought Mary through here, she said something before they silenced her."

"What?" Julianna gasped.

"She said, 'Take the key and go to the cave, at the end--' Then the frigging guard hit her across the face."

"The cave, the key? I don't understand. What does that mean?" she whispered, breaking down in sobs.

"Wait," Lauren whispered. "Didn't Yesie find a way out of the cave?"

"Yes, but why would we go in a cave to find a way out? It doesn't make sense, and why a key?" Julianna looked at Yesie. "What's at the end of the cave, Yesie?"

The small girl looked up into Julianna's eyes, her tear-stained, battered face trying to remember. Then a broad smile spread across her mouth.

"I remember," she whispered. "A light...a beautiful light. A color I've never seen before. It beckoned me in. The light was warm like a thousand arms were hugging me. I felt love. Then I was outside."

Julianna gasped. "Then the men found you?"

"Yes," she quietly said. Her face dropped. "And they brought me here."

"Julianna, it's a portal, a time portal. Doc said the Angel Box emitted the longitude and latitude to him. The portal--it's in the cave," Lauren whispered.

"But how do we get out of here?" Julianna pondered.

She stood up, grasped the rusty bars of the cell door, and shook it violently. It clicked and opened.

She gasped, "Lauren, it's open. The sergeant, he must have done it."

"Blimey. Get to the cave," Lauren whispered.

Julianna looked into the other cells. "Wait, where are Eric and..."

Just then she heard a man scream.

"Lauren, did they take them?" she sobbed.

"Yes," Lauren answered.

Tears stung Julianna's eyes, and she grasped Lauren's hand through the bars.

"I'll find the answer, and I'll come back for all of you."

Lauren nodded her head. Julianna and Yesie ran down the corridor and out into the cool night air. There were no guards in sight as they climbed up the cobblestone steps from the dungeon. They heard the orchestra's music loudly playing in the ballroom and made sure they stayed in the shadows. Then they made a break for it, running in the darkest corners of the vast garden to the cornfield nearby.

The sergeant, he helped us. Not all of them are controlled by her, she thought.

They ran as fast as they could, hiding in the tall rows of corn. A scarecrow in the middle of the field scared them, and they both screamed. Luckily they were far enough away from the mansion that no one heard them. Soon they came to a clearing where an old weeping willow tree stood. There they caught their breathe. In the distance, they could see the mansion's lights glowing. Its grandeur and the beautiful haunting music of the orchestra filled the country side.

Julianna could feel the pulsating of her heart clear up in

her ears as she struggled to calm her nerves. Then she heard water. *A stream*, she thought. She ran towards the sound as Yesie followed. They ran down a steep embankment to a small stream, eagerly cupping their hands and gulping the cool water.

"What way do we go now?" Julianna thought out loud. She soon got her bearings. "This way," she said, grasping Yesie's hand as they began running again.

Soon they came to a small market outside of town. An elderly woman was putting groceries into her car.

"Excuse me, Ma'am. Could we possibly get a ride with you? We've been in an accident, and..."

"Of course, dear," the elderly woman answered, looking them up and down. "Are you alright?"

"Oh, we'll be fine" Julianna replied.

"Don't you need to call the police?"

"Oh...no, that's okay... Um, I don't have insurance. It expired... I didn't realize..." she rambled.

The elderly woman just looked at her.

"The Erickson mansion—can you take us there?"

"Oh, of course, I can," she answered.

"It's right..." Julianna went on.

"Oh dear, everyone know where it is, of course. Get in."

They drove to the mansion. Lights beamed from every window. Julianna thanked the elderly woman, and they ran through the front door. No one was there. Stew was bubbling on the stove, and potatoes were cut up, sitting on the cutting board counter.

"Nellie," Julianna yelled. "Is anyone here?"

She looked in the pantry and kept Yesie close as they ran to every floor screaming for someone, anyone. They were gone. Julianna ran to the kitchen again and opened the desk drawer where Charlotte's car keys were kept. She grabbed Yesie's hand and went past the stove. She turned it off, then spotted the knife sitting by the potatoes and grabbed it and put it in her coat pocket.

Soon Yesie and Julianna were driving towards the old shack where Charlotte had taken them months before. She knew the cave was nearby. Hopefully they could remember and find it again. Yesie was very quiet. Julianna was so intent on getting to their destination she forgot Yesie had never been in a car before. All this was new to her. "Are you alright?"

Yesie nodded her head as she clung to the arm rest.

Soon they approached the gully below the old shack. Julianna drove the Lincoln behind a large thicket, covering it with fallen branches to camouflage it. They used the flashlight from Charlotte's car to run up the path to the shack then past it.

"Yesie, where is it?"

Julianna shined the light all around the forest as they walked.

"It's over there," Yesie pointed, grabbing her hand, pulling her as they made their way to the cave's entrance.

Julianna stood with Yesie in front of the cave, remembering Annabelle's terrifying memory. She looked down at Yesie, imagining how scared she must be to reenter this nightmare. But they had to. They couldn't wait any longer. Anya's guards could be on their trail, and they had to save the others. How she was to do this, she didn't know, but she had to try. She had to go into the cavern again.

"Come on, Yesie. We have to be brave."

They entered once again. The cave was dark, and the entrance was small. They stooped down and crawled for a while. Then the cave got bigger the further down they went.

She shined her light on the cave's walls, seeing moisture dripping from them, and they went down a steep embankment where large boulders lay. Soon the cave leveled off into a small room. This must be where Annabelle hid. She shined her light on the large boulder to the right of her.

"There," Yesie gasped. "The fire was there"

Julianna shined the light where Yesie pointed. Once again, she saw remnants of discarded furniture and charred wood in a pile. Yesie clung tighter to Julianna.

"That's where they did it," she sobbed and buried her face into Julianna's side, sobbing again.

She didn't see skeletons and remembered, "The townspeople buried them."

They quickly walked past into a passageway, then a slow decline. Water dripped on their heads from the ceiling.

We must be under the lake, Julianna thought.

Then they came to the end, a wall.

"What now?"

Then Charlotte's voice--the last thing she said echoed in Julianna's mind. *The key, and Mary said, "Take the key." What key?*

"Yesie, I don't know what they were talking about. Did you have a key when you went through?"

"No, I just put my hands on the wall. I was scared."

"You didn't have a key, and you went through."

She looked at Yesie, shining her light on the battered girls face.

"Kathleen Elizabeth...Yesie, you're the key. It's you."

She hugged Yesie, and then they heard footsteps...a lot of footsteps. The guards were running towards them.

"Anya's men," Julianna whispered.

Yesie went to the wall and started pounding on it with her fist.

Julianna looked back in terror as the lights from the flashlights grew nearer. She also began pounding on the wall. Then a bright light appeared, and it happened just as Yesie had explained. The warmth surrounded them; they felt love then every molecule in their body felt strange…a tingling sensation. Then they were hurling through space. Brilliant lights and stars all around whizzing past them. Then everything slowed down and they were spit out, laying on the other side. They slowly sat up, traumatized trying to figure out their surroundings.

"Where are we?" Julianna whispered.

Everything was gray. Ash was everywhere, as far as they could see. The air was thick with soot. They coughed, trying to clear their lungs.

The landscape they were used to, the lush green grass, rolling hills, trees, beautiful flowers--all gone. All that was left was the burnt out husk of their world. As they trudged through the ash, they saw dead carcasses of animals, deer and cows. They covered their mouths, but the air was thick with soot.

We can't stay here. We'll suffocate. We have to get inside, Julianna thought.

"Let's try to find the car."

They circled back around and found the car, it wouldn't start. Julianna opened the hood and cleared out the air filter. Pretty soon they got the car started and drove to town. The forsaken landscape left little hope of life of any kind. The wood buildings were burnt rubble, and the brick buildings were crumbling with age.

"What year is this?" Julianna wondered.

Yesie looked bewildered and couldn't stop coughing.

Julianna found Charlotte's old scarf in the back seat. She ripped it in two and covered both their noses and mouths, trying to filter out the stagnant air. She knew they couldn't survive much longer, not in these conditions.

"I wonder what happened to everything... Yesie, we have to go back to the cave."

They took a shortcut and drove past the mansion. All that was left of it was rubble. Julianna gasped. It looked like a nuclear bomb had gone off. Every house was completely blown apart. No one could have survived. Everyone must be...dead.

Chapter 36

THEY trudged through the soot which had accumulated. It was at least a foot deep. No matter how hard they tried, it swirled through the air, stinging their eyes and burning their throats. Finally they entered the cave and ran toward the center again. What they saw made Yesie scream in terror, grasping onto Julianna's leg. Julianna couldn't believe her eyes. The cavern that was empty just hours before was filled with corpses.

"It's like they came here to try and survive…of all places," she murmured. Hundreds of dead, decaying bodies covered the floor. The smell was horrendous. Their skin and bodies were burnt. As they stumbled through the carnage, Julianna carried Yesie, who had her head buried in her chest, whimpering. Julianna shined the flashlight on the bodies, trying not to step on them.

What's that? she thought.

It looked like an old newspaper laying under a corpse. She bent down, trying to hold her breath from the stink, and grabbed it. The light from her flashlight started to go out.

"No, not now," she yelled and hit it with her hand, knocking the batteries into place. The light shone bright again, and she could read the article:

> *England is preparing to launch nuclear missiles on the United States along with all other NATO countries. The foreign press has reported there has been no contact with Washington D.C. Reports state that the*

government is no longer in power and fears the worst for the President and his staff. The terrorists' plague is spreading, and many around the world have suffered and perished.

"We have no choice," U.N. officials stated. "Nuclear bombs will be detonated in the near future if terrorists don't surrender. May God be with the people of the United States."

"That was October 29, Oh my God, that's in two weeks," Julianna gasped. "They did it. They nuked us. It's because of Anya. Because of her they destroyed the United States. No!" she screamed and started crying.

Yesie clung tighter to her, and Julianna stood up, dropping the newspaper. They trudged through the scores of bodies, and soon they were standing in front of the wall. Julianna was in shock. Yesie sadly watched as Julianna slouched down and sat across from the wall.

"Julianna, Julianna, please talk to me."

Julianna just sat there, huddled and shivering. Yesie grabbed her arm and dragged her nearer to the wall and started banging on it.

"Please open! Take us out of this wretched place," she cried.

The wall began to vibrate, and soon the warmth enveloped their bodies once again. She dragged Julianna farther into it. Then it swallowed them both into its void, and they traveled back to the past where they had come from.

They lay in the soft wet grass as rain sprinkled down on their faces. Julianna sat up slowly.

"We're back," she gasped and reached up to take off her scarf. Yesie did the same as they breathed in the fresh air. The stars twinkled in the sky as the crescent moon cast its glow on the lush rolling hills.

"That's our future, Yesie, if we don't find a way to stop her," Julianna whispered.

Yesie looked deep into Julianna's eyes. "She's bad. I think she wants it to happen," she said solemnly.

Julianna didn't want to believe that. *What if Yesie is right? What if Anya did want the United States, hell, the whole world destroyed.*

Hell, she thought. *She wants hell on Earth. Oh my God.*

She looked at Yesie as she thought back on what she knew about the Angel Box, the Legend.

"The Angel Box--it's supposedly from God. The devil was cast out of Heaven. He took it and fell to earth, creating a crater which later became the Lake, Erickson Lake. When he hit the ground, he became two, and his counterpart--his daughter--was created."

"The devil's daughter," Yesie said sternly.

"You know about this?" Julianna gasped.

"Everyone knows about it. It's true."

Julianna stared at Yesie. With all this craziness, all the supernatural things that had happened, her logic was starting to disappear. Nothing else made sense, but this did.

"I was at the lake by the Ericksons'," Yesie whispered. "I saw the lady. I heard her singing, and the clicking and chirping. I told my mother, but she told me not to speak of it, that people would think I was a witch. The witches would take children down there," she continued, "and I saw them. They would throw them in the water and she," she started crying, "would feed on them."

Julianna gasped and hugged her.

"The water would get choppy, and there was a light beneath

it, and the noise would get louder... They called her Hawah."
Yesie swallowed the lump in her throat, and she went on. "All
the while the witches would chant, laughing and saying vile
things."

Julianna's mind reeled. She remembered Lady Lavonne and
how she hypnotized and took her back, the video and what
she said about Emily. Emily survived drowning, but she wasn't
Emily; Hawah possessed her.

"The Angel Box--you said the souls of the children were
sucked into it?"

"Yes." Yesie nodded her head.

"So why does Anya want it so badly. Wouldn't it pose a
threat to her?"

"No, she needs its energy."

"Oh, Yesie, we have to go. I think I know how to stop her."

They ran back to the mansion, carefully staying in the
shadows. They saw the stage crew stacking the wood on top
of the mounds of hay, getting it ready for the burning at the
stake scene.

She flashed back to what Doc had said: "Everything had to
be authentic exactly as it was."

Then she remembered there had been a fire. Emily had
been furious. She had chased Victoria up the stairs toward a
bedroom.

"Oh God, Stephen."

She remembered he was locked in that room, and it was
on fire. She remembered him yelling for help. She saw herself
as Victoria banging on the door, and smoke coming out from
under it. Frantically, she started kicking it, trying to break it
down, when all of a sudden someone grabbed her hair. Victoria
whirled around. It was Emily. She had a wild look in her eyes.

Victoria fought back, but Emily was too strong. She pushed her down the stairs just as her father, Mr. Erickson, ran in. He witnessed the entire scene. Furious, he ran up the stairs and grabbed Emily. She fought him and broke away. Then part of the ceiling collapsed, crushing and killing him in a fiery blaze. Then Doc ran in and carried Victoria out

He saved me, she thought.

"My dad and Stephen died," she gasped and looked at Yesie. "She's going to try to recreate it. We can't let her."

Then Julianna whispered to Yessie the plan that would impact their lives forever. It had to work, or all would be lost, and the world as they knew it was doomed. Yesie's eyes grew large as she listened to Julianna's plan, then she set off to gather what she needed.

Behind Julianna, the orchestra's haunting melody filled the night air, and the mansion's lights glowed from its enormous etched windows. She watched as the dancers waltzed mechanically like puppets inside. All were controlled by Anya. She quickly gathered what she needed. She felt the knife in her coat pocket and tied the rope loosely around her waist. Yesie came crawling back silently through the thick shrubbery.

"Did you get everything?" Julianna whispered.

"I think so," Yesie quietly replied.

"Let's hope this works," Julianna murmured.

Chapter 37

A shriek went up from the dance floor as Anya's shrill voice echoed throughout the building. The orchestra stopped abruptly.

"What! You fools! You didn't find her."

Then there was a horrible crash. Tables and chairs started flying through the air as Anya's kinetic powers turned the beautiful room into shambles. The actors and cast members came running out, most of them bloody. Anya's guards started swarming out the doors with their guns drawn, flashing lights while scanning the grounds. Julianna grabbed Yesie and hid in the thickets down behind the rose garden, where the bonfires were to be set.

In the rose garden, they saw that Mary, Anna, and Mrs. Hastings were being lead out, hands tied behind their backs. The other guards frantically searched for Julianna and Yesie.

The guards tied Mary to a post high atop the woodpile while Anya watched.

"You must have front row seats. You mustn't miss this," she said dryly to Annabelle and Mrs. Hastings as guards strapped them to a fence.

Anya's eyes glistened with pleasure. Then the guards placed a burlap bag over Mary's head, as her mother and sister looked on in horror. But she wasn't the only one tied to the stakes; four others were shackled with her: Professor Hilard, Lauren, Nellie and Carlos. Julianna cried out in horror when she saw them. Luckily the orchestra music had started again, so no one heard her but Yesie. Yesie looked sadly up at Julianna and squeezed her hand tightly. Julianna hugged her. How on earth were they going to save them all? Her plan was to just save Mary from the fire. She needed more help.

Just then she saw the sergeant getting closer. He was searching through the bushes with a flashlight. Yesie hunched down further into the thicket as he trudged pass them, almost stepping on her. The other guards left after securing the four atop the wood pile, and Anya had gone back into the mansion along with the guards. She could hear Nellie and Lauren screaming for help. All the while the sergeant still searched silently by himself. Julianna knew he was their only chance. He had left the cell door open. Maybe Anya didn't control him. If there was a remote ounce of humanity left inside him, she had to take that chance. If not all would be lost.

"Sergeant Thomas, Sergeant Thomas."

He stopped abruptly and turned his flashlight on them. They sat huddled in the thicket, the light blinding them as they pleaded with him. He put a whistle on a chain around his neck up to his mouth and started to blow, but then suddenly stopped as he stared at their pathetic faces. Seeing Julianna jolted him back to reality. What was he doing? He'd been walking around for days in a trance listening and doing everything Anya ordered. She had his wife and children and threatened him with their lives. But he couldn't do this. He couldn't hurt these innocent people. The whistle dropped from his mouth.

"We need your help" Julianna pleaded.

He bent down and whispered, "She has my family."

Julianna understood. She nodded and squeezed his hand. "Do you know where the Angel Box is?"

"Yes, she has it in her room in a safe," he answered. "Please, you have to get it, but don't touch it. Wrap something around your hands."

"I'll try," he said.

Then he turned and sprinted behind the mansion, making sure Anya didn't see him going up the back stairs to the bedroom. She was busily talking to the director and didn't notice.

First, Julianna crawled over to Annabelle and Mrs. Hastings, cutting the ropes from their shackled wrists.

"Don't move from this spot. They can't know," she whispered.

They watched as Julianna and Yesie put their plan to work, freeing Mary and hoisting the scarecrow up onto where she had been, tying it in place and putting the burlap sack over its head. Julianna quickly went and cut the rope from the ankles and wrists of the others.

"Where are Mr. Erickson, Eric and Doc?" Julianna whispered.

"I don't know," Lauren sobbed. "The guards took them first. I don't know where they are."

"You need to go now" Julianna whispered, and they ran to the cornfield to hide.

Where's Eric? she thought. *Will I ever see him again?* She couldn't think about that now. She had work to do.

Chapter 38

THE music suddenly stopped again. Anya, the director, and film crew walked towards them. Yesie was in the corn-field with everyone else.

"Stay there," Julianna gestured. She saw smoke from the mansion. Then there was a big explosion. The film crew was filming the entire time as Anya hurried the crew towards the woodpile. Fire erupted from the back of the mansion.

"Just like before," Julianna gasped. *Eric. Where's Eric?* Her heart stopped. Panicked, she ran as fast as she could towards the mansion. Meanwhile, Anya made it to the woodpile and told her guards to light the fire. Anya soon realized, as the blaze lit up the darkness, the others were gone. The fire immediately torched the scarecrow, and she understood that it wasn't Mary. Letting out a scream of rage, she raced back into the mansion as the camera crew ran after her. She saw Julianna at the top of the stairs banging frantically on the bedroom door. She could hear Eric calling for help from inside.

Anya levitated up the stairs, grabbing Julianna by the hair and tearing her away from the door. Then Anya jumped on her, slamming her to the ground. She revealed the truly evil being she was, scratching and biting Julianna in a fit of rage, then she threw her down the stairs. Julianna's body lay limp, bloody, and broken at the bottom. The director and camera crew realized this was not acting; this was insanity. They took their cameras and fled.

Mr. Erickson ran in as Anya catapulted from the top of the stairs and ran out the door. He saw Julianna lying at the bottom unconscious. As he bent down to help her, he heard Eric's screams for help. He ran upstairs. The building was filling with smoke. He pounded on the door, then began ramming it with his body...to no avail.

Dr. Swenson ran in and saw Julianna lying helplessly at the bottom of the stairs. Then he heard Mr. Erickson slamming his body into the door above him. The crackling of the fire was getting closer; he felt the heat singe his skin. The smoke was thick, and he began coughing. He must get Julianna out. As he picked her up, he heard the mansion creak and groan as Mr. Erickson relentlessly continued slamming against the door, determined to save Eric. Then part of the roof collapsed, crushing Mr. Erickson in a fiery blaze.

Dr. Swenson was horrified. He knew he had to get out quickly with Julianna. He ran for the door as debris fell all around him, finally making it outside as the mansion erupted into a blazing inferno.

Anya's bedroom was full of smoke. Sargeant Thomas entered from a back window where he found Eric tied to a chair and cut him loose. He tried to open the safe but the smoke and fire were too much for them. They had to leave quickly or perish. Mr. Erickson's body lay dead under the debris as the flames licked at his body. The actors and crew stood outside watching as the mansion went up in flames, still thinking it was a terrible accident, and finally coming out of the trance they'd all been under.

The crows began to swarm in huge flocks perching in the

trees. Then the wolves and rats appeared and roamed freely around the frightened actors. Anya ran to Annabelle and Mrs. Hastings. She grabbed Annabelle's arm, nearly breaking it.

"Where is she? Where's Mary?" she snarled, her beauty gone.

All that remained was a bent over hag. She flung Annabelle across the rose garden. Annabelle landed hard on the ground, not moving, as the wolves and rats surrounded her bloody body. Mrs. Hastings ran to her sobbing. The spell was broken and the wolves, crows, and rats began to change into their true forms, the hideous creatures that they really were. The witches also regained their powers. Yesie peered through the bushes as the witches descended toward Annabelle and her mother.

Then, as if time stopped, Mary walked out of the blazing mansion carrying the Angel Box. Doc had lain Julianna down on a bench, the furthest from the blaze. Eric ran to her side. She woke up and saw Mary walking stoically towards her mother and sister. She was glowing, as was the Angel Box, and the witches' powers were useless against her. The witches parted as she walked through them towards Anya and her family. Anya trembled in fear, her bent over, haggard body aging rapidly. She was afraid of Mary.

Mary bent down to her sister and placed the Angel Box by her side. Then Mary lovingly and gently stroked Annabelle's hair.

Julianna slowly sat up. Everything ached in her body. She grabbed Eric's hand and kissed him. Then they watched as Annabelle stood up, and the family embraced each other, then formed a circle around the Box, grabbing hands.

The witches began to back up, frightened, as Mary and her family raised their hands high into the dark night chanting.

Yahweh, Yahweh
evil shall die
All the souls release
to the sky.
Devil's Daughter
Demons below
Never return, this promise
Bestow.

Then with a touch of their clasped hands to the Angel Box a bright light emanated, then engulfed them, and millions of tiny souls descended into the night.

Julianna and Eric watched in astonishment, as did the others. Mary and her family evaporated into light as well and disappeared into the darkness.

"No," Julianna screamed, trying to run toward them as Doc and Eric held her back.

The witches screeched as they melted into the ground, leaving nothing but a putrid, gooey, black liquid. Anya started screaming in agony as Yesie ran to Julianna, clutching her tightly, burying her head in her shoulder, shaking and sobbing.

Anya kept screaming as she withered and slowly died. Then they heard a loud clicking and chirping coming from the lake as it bubbled and boiled. The water receded, leaving only an empty hole.

Lauren, Nellie, Carlos, and Professor Hilard ran from the cornfield towards them, breathless. They all stood in shock, traumatized at what they'd seen.

The film crew and director started coming out of the trance they'd been under. They watched in awe, standing silently with the rest.

Eric and Julianna, while holding on to Yesie's hand, walked

hesitantly toward the Angel Box as it sat untarnished in the middle of the carnage. They slowly walked over to where Anya's remains lay. The black, slimy mound suddenly moved, and they jumped back.

Doc saw it too. "Listen," he said.

There was a soft whimpering. He took a stick and carefully jabbed at her dead remains, splitting them open. Something moved inside. He bent down as the others stepped back. Doc couldn't believe what he was seeing. A small body was moving. It was a child, a child covered with the remains of evil. It started coughing and sputtering.

"Doc, don't touch it," Eric yelled.

But Doc couldn't resist. He carefully helped the small child sit up. She was covered in the black tar-like substance. All that showed was her big emerald eyes staring up at him. He gasped.

"Doc?" a small voice emerged. "Doc is it you?"

"Yes, my Dear."

He bent down and wiped the black slime off her face. Then embraced her, sobbing uncontrollably.

Julianna and the rest of them stood awestruck. Doc turned towards them holding the child in his arms.

"Everyone--" He cleared his throat. "I'd like to introduce you to someone who was once very dear to me... This is Emily, Emily Erickson."

Everyone was shocked and stepped backwards, all except Julianna. Her mind jolted back to the birthday party at the lake, the soft billowy clouds floating in the clear blue sky, her sister's musical laughter as they ran through the fields of tall grass and bright wild flowers, how much she'd loved her… That love never died. Her love would live on for eternity.

Julianna walked up to Emily as Yesie clung to Eric's leg.

She reached out her hand to Emily, and Emily grabbed it back. Then they stared into each other's eyes.

"Hello, Emily. I'm Julianna." "Pleased to meet you," she shyly said.

ACKNOWLEDGEMENTS

1st Draft – Heather Rau
1st & 2nd Edit – Jennifer Flath
Book Cover – taylor luke DESIGNS

YAUNA HANSEN-SMITH

Yauna Hansen-Smith lives in Vancouver, WA, with her husband Steve. She has three children and four grandchildren. Yauna has been writing for thirteen years, and also has a career as a choreographer and dance teacher. This is her first published work. "*The Angel Box*" is the first in the series and the second book; "*The Pentacle*" will be released in the Spring of 2015.

CPSIA information can be obtained
at www.ICGtesting.com
Printed in the USA
FFOW02n1808220418
46300059-47802FF

9 780578 150833